DEDICATION

*To the amazing authors who invited
me to join them in this fascinating project:
Deb, Peg, Vicki, Regan, and Rita –
thank you so much for including me
on this wonderful journey.*

*Hugs,
Cindy*

CONTENTS

SNOW BLIND

PROLOGUE

ROME, Italy
   June, 18 months ago

JOSH HASKINS MANEUVERED her royal high-brow, Princess Anastasia Gerhardt – aka: Ms. Blond, beautiful and bratty – firmly behind him and away from the pack of bar lizards, fending them off as he backed toward the alley exit of the mobbed party bar.

True to form, the princess had dragged him into the middle of the obscenely rich and spoiled Italian jet set scene, dressed like a designer slut in her lipstick red mini dress and attracting every stray dog and lone wolf with a yen to howl.

"This is so bogus," he muttered beneath a grinding rock beat and a full on testosterone blast. They came at her like worker drones flocking to the queen bee. No one, however, was allowed to taste her honey. Not on his watch.

Good Lord. *This* was his first official, full-fledged assignment as a Rapid Response Alliance operative? Was he hunting terrorists in the middle of the Congo? Running recon on a

1

snatch and grab op in the Middle East? Even guarding a diplomatic cadre to a top secret security meeting? Oh, hell, no.

His first *mission* was to: A) keep the princess happy, B) keep the princess safe, and C) keep the princess from creating an international incident.

At the moment, C was giving him the most trouble. That and his simmering temper.

"You don't want to do this," Josh warned as an inebriated Romeo, stunning in a black, silk shirt opened to his navel, a boatload of bling hanging around his neck, and skin-tight do-you-like-my-package leather pants, separated himself from the pack and made a move toward the princess.

The wannabe paramour took one look at the dark rage on Josh's face and thought better of his decision. Not so drunk after all, Josh was happy to report. The problem was, at least ten other contenders were circling the campfire, ready to take a crack at roasting Anastasia's marshmallows.

"It wasn't enough that you had to incite a riot in that almost dress," he sputtered to her royal pain-in-the ass. "You had to hop up on the bar. Had to pour champagne down your cleavage and invite every Tom, Dick, and Horny to come and lick it off."

Behind him, Anastasia giggled. "A girl's gotta have fun."

Josh glanced over his shoulder and glared into flirty, fiery, blue eyes. Blue like a summer sky he'd thought the first time he'd seen them. Ha. Blue like the color his balls were gonna be if he didn't get her out of this den of dickwads and soon.

He ducked a flying beer bottle, shoved the princess more securely behind him, and swore to God that if he got her out of this mess without creating that international incident she was bent on making, he was going to throw her over his knee and whale the tar out of her sexy little behind. PC or not.

"So help me God, Ant*ipasto*," he grumbled as he held back

2

the pack crocked on vino and hell bent on tasting the Princess's bountiful cleavage, "when I get you back to the hotel, we're going to have us a little come to Jesus meeting."

"Sounds positively … spiritual," the princess of the newly sovereign nation of Slarovia purred into his ear in perfect English as she dug red lacquered nails that matched her dress deeper into his shoulders.

She squealed then ducked behind him when a particularly brave — read: stupid — admirer made a grab at her. A quick chop to his arm and a well-placed knee to his breadbasket dispensed with Stupid.

Another one bites the dust.

The floor was already littered with the guys' 'brothers in rut' who'd thought they were going to worship at the altar of the ultimate one night stand.

Another bottle flew by just as Josh made it to the exit and backed the princess through the door and into a heat drenched Italian night pungent with the scents of garlic and wine and trouble.

Man, this sucked. Josh Haskins had never quit on anything in his life, yet five bullet-sweating, tongue-biting days into this assignment watch dogging the high-maintenance, party animal, Anastasia, and saving her blue-blooded hide from one scrape after another, and he was ready to cash in his chips.

"Babysitter. That's all I am. A glorified babysitter," he grumbled as he dragged her away from the bar at a brisk clip and finally left the wannabe bad boys behind.

Pale street lights and a rumbling rock beat leaked out of the bar, following them as he hustled her down the narrow, cobblestone strada.

"Slow down, would you? I can't run in these heels."

He ignored her sputtering protests and tried to remember

why he'd agreed to this assignment. Oh, yeah. Something about saving the world.

Well, hell, what red-blooded American patriot could resist a stab at doing just that? He'd been born for the job. Or so complained any woman who had ever gotten too close and thought she might have a chance of taking over as the number one priority in his life.

So, no. Josh hadn't been able to resist. When he'd finally received the invitation to join RRA and had been offered this cock-eyed assignment, he'd have said yes to latrine duty.

"Yes, sir, I'm up for anything, sir." Even though it meant that Josh's rookie run as a new recruit for the elite and clandestine international organization involved playing bodyguard to a spoiled brat of a newly minted European princess.

"I said, slow down!" The princess demanded, putting on the skids.

Satisfied that they were well clear of the nightclub, Josh stopped, turned and glared at five feet six inches of cover girl curves and cascading blond hair. Who could blame those poor Casanovas? This woman put the sex in sex appeal. She also put the Tick in ticked off – which he was. Royally.

"You know," Josh said, nailing her with a look, "if you had the sense God gave a goat, I wouldn't have to drag you out of one scrape after another."

"Not up to the assignment, Haskins?"

Baiting him? She was actually *baiting* him? After all the crap he'd put up with in the last five days?

"Fine. Have your fun," he ground out as the knot at the end of his rope finally unraveled. "Only from now you can have it without me. I've had it with this gig."

And he'd had it with the woman, who, despite her princess to peasant regard for him, somehow managed to rile both his anger and his testosterone levels to new heights. Did. Not. Compute.

4

"Come on." He latched on to her wrist and stormed off again, as angry at her as he was at himself for letting her sex-goddess looks get to him. "I'm taking you back to the hotel. Then we're going to see about getting you a new babysitter. I'm officially turning in my nanny badge."

Hell. He'd thought that once he'd made the grade, cracked the RRA requirements and become an operative that he'd be knee deep in international espionage.

So much for what he'd thought.

Slowly, Josh became aware that she was laughing.

Laughing.

He stopped – and she ran smack into him. He latched on to both arms to steady her then set her none too gently away. "So happy to entertain you."

"Oh, you do." Her grin widened. "I wondered how hard I was going to have to push you before you finally snapped."

He glared at the top of her head. She'd started tugging off her sky high stilettos.

"Sweet heaven, that feels good." Standing bare-foot on the cobblestones, she tossed both shoes over her shoulder into a hedge, giving them a good ride.

He looked from the flying heels back to her face. "*How hard you were going to have to push to finally make me snap?*"

"Oh, for Pete's sake, Haskins. Lighten up. You passed, okay? And none too soon for my taste. I was running out of stunts."

He waited three beats, watching her eyes as she dragged a tumble of hair away from her face. "What the hell are you talking about?"

"Okay," she said conversationally, like he wasn't glaring daggers and contemplating wrapping his hands around that lovely slim neck and wringing it until her tongue turned as blue as her eyes.

"Here's the deal, Haskins. I was a test."

5

Another three beat pause while he watched her with ever narrowing eyes. "A test."

"Well, *Anastasia* was a test. For me too, if it's any consolation. In fact, there is no such animal – or in this case no such *party* animal."

She smiled.

He didn't.

"Lieutenant Cara Graves, European base, RRA Headquarters, Barcelona. And you were my cross to bear as much as Anastasia was yours."

He felt his temperature rise right along with his hackles. "Cross to bear?"

She sighed. "As you may have surmised by now, I'm not a princess. My name is not Anastasia Gehart-"

"Got that part," he said through his clenched jaw.

"I'm an RRA operative who was given the assignment of testing your mettle ten ways from Sunday to make certain you were up for any task – even one as seemingly trivial and demeaning as babysitting a brat.

"So cool your jets, Haskins," she added, not even a tiny bit rattled when he continued to glare bullets at her. "Just settle down and congratulate yourself on a job well done."

She extended her hand. "You've passed muster. Welcome aboard."

Duped. He'd been duped like a UN weapons inspector.

He ignored her hand. "This was all a set up?"

She shrugged. "Call it an initiation. Someday, I might tell you what they did to initiate me." She smiled again and tried for another handshake.

"I don't give a damn what they did to you." He spun around and headed for the hotel. "You and RRA can take your muster and your initiation and stick it where the sun don't shine."

"Hmmm. Never said you were a poor sport on your application."

He flipped her the bird and kept walking.

"You *really* want to miss your first *real* field assignment?" she called after him.

Josh stopped, turned, glared at her where she stood in a pool of light cast from a street lantern. Golden hair a gorgeous, messy tangle. Blue eyes challenging and amused. The thin strap of her short, slinky red dress, sliding off her left shoulder.

For an instant, he had to remind himself how ticked off he was. "Oh. A *real* assignment?" he spat sarcastically. "What? The queen of England due for a party run and needs a driver?"

The husky sound of her laugh had something other than his anger rising again.

"Oh, it's waaay better than that."

He considered her with enough skepticism to fill the Coliseum. "It had better be."

She'd walked closer and in a low and deadly serious voice told him.

Good. God. It was good all right. As good as it got.

TWELVE HOURS later
Barcelona, Spain

JOSH WAITED PATIENTLY in the dimly lit situation room; adrenaline mainlined directly into his blood stream; his tension peaked right along with his curiosity. His ALICE pack sat on the floor beside his M4 assault rifle. He was pumped and ready for this mission. His first real mission with RRA.

And he was ready to meet his new CO. A fellow warrior – not a smart mouthed wasp of an agent who played the role of diva far too well.

Initiation my ass. Damn, he was glad to be free of Anastasia ... make that Cara, he corrected with a grunt. He'd had enough of both of them, thank you very much.

He checked his watch. Less than a quarter of an hour until they deployed. The assignment was plum, as she'd promised: Infiltrate an outer island off the Malaysian coast and the hideout of the terrorist cell, Death Toll. Find the plant that produced lethal nerve gas then neutralize and destroy both the facility and the stockpile of the deadly poison. Added bonus: Capture or eliminate the terrorists responsible.

Piece of cake, he thought with a grim look at the terrain map tacked to the wall and hoped his lawyer had finished the last minute changes to his will. If anything happened to him, he wanted his nephew taken care of.

A door opened behind him. Josh snapped to attention without turning around. Only one other person had clearance for this room at this hour. His new CO.

"At ease, Sergeant."

Josh stopped breathing. Was pretty sure his heart stopped beating, too.

He knew that voice. What he didn't know, was why he was hearing it now.

"I said at ease."

He turned slowly as Lieutenant Cara Graves walked into the room, combat ready in jungle camos, M16 in hand, a modified ALICE pack strapped to her back.

"What the hell are you doing here?" Josh finally managed when he could get his mouth to work.

"Wanna rephrase that, Sergeant?"

Josh swallowed, eyes dead ahead as Lt. Graves moved to stand directly in front of him.

"What the hell are you doing here, *sir*?" he repeated crisply.

But deep in his gut, he already knew. Damn it all to hell, he knew.

"You got a problem working with a female operative, Haskins?"

He had a problem working with *this* female operative.

"No, sir," he gritted out, knowing that if he voiced his objections he'd be off the op faster than you could say, *You blew it, buddy*.

"Got a problem with a female outranking you?"

Lord, help him.

"No, sir."

"Good answer."

Oh, she knew he was ticked.

"Good." She headed for the door. "Then grab your gear. Transport bird's waiting to take us to the Philippines. And pull the bug out of your butt, sergeant. Let's go save the world."

CEDAR RAPIDS 9 NEWS

December 22
1:20 pm

"Remember that you heard it here first folks."

Don McDowell flashed pearly white teeth to the camera and stacked his pages of copy on the desk in front of him. "KCRG TV 9 first alert weather is not afraid to predict that the Cedar Rapids viewing area is either going to dodge a major bullet or we're going to get hit with potentially the most massive winter blizzard seen in this area in almost a century."

Julie Paul, the evening anchor, gave Don a comical smile. "Wow, Don. Could you *be* any more ambiguous?"

Don chuckled and the camera followed the weatherman as he rose from his desk and moved in front of an Iowa weather map swirling with radar simulations, snowflakes and as an added humorous touch, question marks.

"I couldn't be more vague if I tried, Julie. Let me try to explain why the forecast is such a mystery."

Don manipulated the map with the touch of his finger to

include several western and northern states as well as the southern part of Canada. "Many of you have been aware of Blizzard Holly, whose genesis was in Canada before she swooped down into Montana, Colorado, back up to Nebraska, then east into South Dakota."

He turned back to face the camera. "Holly is currently blasting Minnesota and all indications are that she has no predilection to blow herself out anytime soon. Based on the route she's taken she may – or may not," he added with a smile of caution, "find her way down through east central Iowa.

"Why, you might ask, can't I be more specific? Well, there are so many variables in play as of now that even the National Weather Service's state of the art computers can't pinpoint the storm's path or its full effect on Iowa. Forecast details will become clearer and more accurate as this blizzard keeps churning through Minnesota.

"Those variables include a low pressure system here." He used a hand-held remote to zero in on the map. "The jet stream over here, upper level winds, and how much cold air is in place when, or if, the storm arrives. Even a relatively small change in this low pressure system, for instance, can make a huge difference. A shift one way can create blizzard conditions while the other way could bring only a light dusting of snow."

His expression became serious. "Here at TV 9, we realize how critical it is for you all to know what weather you may be facing in the near future. It's almost Christmas, after all. Many of you have travel plans or family planning to visit you. For that reason, we're taking a very cautious approach to predicting the effect Holly will have on our viewing area."

The camera moved in for a close up. "Rest assured, we are monitoring this storm like NASA monitors a rocket launch. We'll cut into regular programming if necessary to keep you up to date on Holly's path and velocity and the severity of the snowfall, the wind and the cold.

"In the meantime, look for cloudy skies tomorrow with a high of twenty-three degrees Fahrenheit and north winds no more than five miles per hour. Sunrise will be at 7:31am and we should have a beautiful sunset at 4:38pm.

"Have a great rest of your evening and all day tomorrow. Julie – back to you…"

CHAPTER ONE

T'WAS THE SEASON. Family. Friends. Food. Ho. Ho. Ho. The team was definitely due for some R & R. They weren't going to get it. Not yet. At least Cara wasn't. Neither, she'd decided, was Haskins.

Another flight announcement over the din of the crowds waiting at Chicago, O'Hare, Terminal C, had her rising wearily to her feet.

"That's us." Cara shouldered her carry-on and got in line with the passengers boarding the December 23rd, 12:10 pm flight from Chicago, to Cedar Rapids, Iowa.

Her Christmas holiday. Not how Cara had seen it playing out. The RRA jet had delivered them from NYC to Chicago an hour ago but it was commercial from here on in. They didn't want to draw any undue attention. A private Gulfstream flying into the small airport in Cedar Rapids this close to Christmas probably wouldn't raise any red flags but it could draw some speculative attention and that was the last thing they wanted.

Keeping a low profile was already a bit tricky considering that Haskins drew the interest of most women and a few envious men. It was human nature. When you saw a six foot four, ruggedly attractive, mature male who could easily pose for the cover of MEN's HEALTH magazine, it was hard not to stare. Especially when his gaze landed, even briefly, on you. Steel gray. Piercing. Aged to perfection from creases fed by the sun and combat and living on the edge.

So low profile? Not so much. Not with Haskins on the scene. Still, it was economy seats and a valiant attempt at playing average Jane and Joe. Carry on only. There hadn't been time for packing so they'd each brought only specific technical surveillance gadgetry that they'd need and couldn't buy when they got there. RRA had provided them both with night vision glasses equipped with infrared thermal imaging cameras. As far as she knew, they were the first to field test this new version.

Otherwise, if they needed anything else they'd have to buy it locally. And hope everything wasn't sold out this close to Christmas. Guess they'd soon find out.

Icy air stung Cara's cheeks, making her eyes water as they crossed the open tarmac toward the small airbus that would deliver them to Cedar Rapids in under an hour.

Haskins, a North Carolina boy, tucked his chin into the collar of his jacket but didn't grumble about the cold. Haskins never grumbled. He glared. He simmered. Sometimes, he even boiled. But like a good soldier, he followed orders and did his job. Did it with precision and skill and if he had a problem with her performance as the team leader and as his CO, he hadn't shown it on a single one of their many missions during the last year and a half.

He clearly, however, had a problem with her. With being

around her. With sometimes being very near to her in the often close confines required by their operations.

She wasn't mistaken about that. She felt something. The crackle. The sizzle. Even the occasional fissure in his concentration. And none of it had anything to do with his test as Anastasia's baby sitter. No. This had nothing to do with Anastasia and everything to do with Cara Graves.

Aware of him walking with purpose across the tarmac behind her, she kept her eyes dead ahead, shivering against the brutal cold as she climbed the open jet stairs. In her experience, there weren't many places colder than a flat, windy tarmac in the middle of winter.

She quickly found her seat in the sixty-passenger air bus and dropped heavily into it. Low on sleep from the scramble to make this mission, she was determined to at least catch a power nap on the hour long flight.

The flight to Iowa. A flyover state. Corn, if she remembered right. Cows. Oh, yeah. And a state fair made famous in the vintage movie Music Man and for a cow made of butter. Homeland, USA. Not exactly a hotbed of terrorist activity. Cold as a freezer the end of December – just like it was in Chicago, NYC, and Boston.

She had high hopes that with any luck, this would be a quick recon mission. They'd be in and out. Twenty-four hours max. Then she'd head back to Boston in time for Christmas dinner at her sister's. She had big plans to gorge herself on pumpkin pie, zone out to the crackling of an apple wood fire, and watch her gorgeous five year old twin nieces plow into the presents she'd brought them.

Sometimes she wanted that. Home, hearth, kids and a dog. Yeah, especially around the holidays, she questioned her dangerous and solitary career choice. But then a mission would come up. The adrenaline would start rushing through her bloodstream and she knew why she did what she did.

Someday. Maybe. While she was still young enough to have children and not too old to learn how to cook.

Smiling at herself for lapsing into a bit of melancholy, she stowed her gear under the seat, buckled herself in and closed her eyes, peripherally aware of Haskins buckling in across the aisle.

His broad shoulders and long legs over-filled the skimpy seat. She didn't have to look at him to know that his steely gray eyes betrayed no emotion. As usual. The man was a bit of an enigma. And she found him a bit too interesting. That was all going to change.

Right now, she needed that power nap. If she was lucky, she'd be asleep before the landing gear tucked into the belly of the jet. But instead of sleeping, she found herself thinking about Haskins again.

Why had she chosen him for this mini mission? Well, not exactly chosen. He'd volunteered like a good team member so the others could enjoy their holiday with family. Which worked out fine because if he hadn't stepped up, she'd been going to tap him for the op anyway.

She'd decided it was time to admit that she had a little problem with him. A problem a commanding officer didn't need with a subordinate. A problem that was universally wrong under any operational circumstances.

This was her chance to confront and dissuade said problem before anything out of order happened between them. To face and conquer it without interference from the team. That's why she'd wanted just the two of them on this low risk, low adrenaline recon. Cooler minds do prevail. She needed to clear the air because if she didn't, she was afraid she knew where this was heading. Sex. Maybe even something more.

Sex and work didn't mix. Especially with their kind of work. Life and death situations didn't allow for even minor slip ups that a distracting physical relationship could possibly initiate.

You didn't think with your head when you were involved with someone whose life was on the line. Made stupid decisions based on emotions instead of logic. Took stupid chances.

So, yes. It was time to sort it out with him. Admit that the attraction wasn't just on his end. Agree that they needed to face it, forget it, and forge on without acting on their more primal urges which, without a doubt, could jeopardize their future missions.

So she'd fix it. Nip it in the bud.

Satisfied that her secondary mission to clear the air with Haskins was a go, she fell asleep.

Yet as she slept, she dreamed. Unfortunately, Haskins was in the dream. Again.

Naked.

Again.

———

THE EASTERN IOWA airport was small but modern and efficient. As soon as they disembarked the plane, they rode down the single escalator and headed straight toward the rental car counters.

"Better get a 4-wheel drive," Cara said, otherwise deferring the rest of the details to Haskins to select their ride.

Outside the terminal windows, a light mix of freezing rain and snow had started falling. She didn't like the looks of that but since she couldn't do anything about it, she turned to her GPS to acquaint herself with the Cedar Rapids area.

Five minutes later, Haskins met her by the exit door pocketing a set of keys.

"Everyone had the same idea," he said.

She looked up as he held out the paperwork for the rental.

"Best I could do is a small SUV. Let's hope it's got good traction. And did we know we were running into snow?"

She let out air between puffed cheeks. "Weather reports have been sketchy. Last I heard, the snow was going to veer back north but, apparently, we're getting a little Christmas surprise. Let's regroup on the road and hope we're in and out before the worst of the weather sets in."

After cleaning the dusting of snow off their white SUV, they stowed their bags in the back seat and Haskins settled in behind the wheel.

"Head north toward I-380. We've got a little ways to go."

"Read me in," he said, as they cleared the airport parking complex.

Need to know was standard mission protocol and up until this moment, Haskins hadn't had a clue what they were about.

"Palo, Iowa, about twenty minutes north of here, is the site of an aging nuclear energy plant."

"Still in use?" He flipped the turn signal and pulled out onto the on ramp.

"As of now, yes. It's due to close in the next year or so, though. This plant has been in commission since the 70's so obviously it's got some years on it. In any event," she continued then caught a gasp when the SUV hit an icy patch and fishtailed sideways.

"Sorry." Haskins let off the gas, regained control and they continued on their way.

Windshield wipers worked at slapping away the snow that had picked up a little in intensity. The defrost fan ran overtime to keep the glass fog free.

"In any event," Cara began again, relieved to scc that Haskins had regained a solid handle on the vehicle, "RRA received a report from NSA. They intercepted a burst of cyber-chatter from an IP address in Cedar Rapids. This was a week ago."

"And this nuc plant was mentioned," he concluded.

"Actually, no." She smiled grimly. "The plant was never mentioned, but Armageddon was - several times. Along with some veiled phrases that are typical of extremist groups wanting to make a big noise about a big bang.

"Before NSA could zero in on absolutes, though, whoever was communicating using this IP address got wise and started encrypting all of their messages. Then, two days ago, they went totally silent."

"Which raised some red flags," Haskins deduced. "Still a stretch to think we're going to find Armageddon in the making. From locals. In Iowa."

"Apparently this same IP user had been on their radar a couple of years ago for much of the same kind of chatter but went silent then, too."

"Until last week when they picked up this new communication. Still," he said, sounding dubious. "Like I said. It's a stretch."

"True. But stranger things have happened," she reminded him.

"Yeah. 9-11," Haskins mulled grimly. "Seems I remember a connection to one of the hijackers and Cedar Rapids."

"There was that," she agreed quietly and felt the overwhelming rush of anger and anguish and patriotism that had been the impetus for her Army enlistment and ultimately her service in the RRA.

She'd been a kid when the Towers fell, but she'd never forget the images on TV and the utter despair she'd felt for the victims and the country. Her future had been decided then and there. She wanted to serve. She *needed* to serve and her focus from that moment on was doing just that. As soon as she turned eighteen, she joined the Army, worked her way up to a noncom officer, furthered her education and advanced through both the service and her degrees to her position at RRA.

She'd led missions all over the world. Asia. Soviet Union. Iraq, Syria, Afghanistan, Central America. There wasn't a Third World or sophisticated European country where she hadn't laid down footprints.

Now? Now she was in Iowa. The thought that she was within driving distance to the Field of Dreams as opposed to the killing fields of Cambodia made her smile. She was due for a cush assignment. She was banking on this sneak and peep being it.

Beside her, Haskins drove in thoughtful silence. She took the time to pull up the RRA message on her phone and reread the directive in case she'd missed anything. The orders had been short on info and long on speculation. Because of that sudden flurry of cyber-chatter over a very recent and very brief window of time, NSA alerted RRA to scramble together a team and check things out immediately.

Everything had moved at warp speed after that. They'd been wheels up out of LaGuardia within two hours of their return from their most recent mission in Somalia. Just the two of them. Traveling light and lean while Christmas travelers hummed along with the holiday music piped over the airport PA system between called and canceled flights.

She closed the message and stared out at the interstate which had become a ribbon of white. "Let's hope it's a wild goose chase."

"Your Christmas wish?"

She smiled. "Close enough."

They both knew that at any given time, there were details similar to theirs checking out threats, sometimes finding nothing, sometimes squashing a real menace that the general public would never hear anything about.

"The life of a shadow warrior," Haskins said with a self-effacing smile. "Missed holidays, missed opportunities. Nothing but selflessness and sacrifice."

"Yeah, that," Cara said, appreciating this little glimpse of his sense of humor – something she'd rarely seen. "Regardless, whoever these people are, we need to find out if they're some wannabe bad guys just talking to hear themselves talk or if they're the real deal and they're actually planning something."

"How did NSA settle on this nuc plant as the likely target?"

"Process of elimination. There are other potential targets in the area, yes, but none as target rich and as capable of producing death and destruction as this."

"Got it. So has security at the nuc plant been notified?"

"Not yet. No need getting everyone's tail in a twist if it turns out to be a false alarm."

He nodded. "So we're strictly recon and assessment."

"That's the directive, yes. We need to get a read on: a) if we're truly looking at a terrorist cell, b) and if so, if they're actually planning something - which would most likely be destruction or damage to the plant, c) if they have a plan, how far developed it is, and d) if they have the means to pull it off."

He grunted, tapped his thumbs on the wheel. "And it had to be at Christmas. Of course."

"If we're looking at jihadists, then yes. It's the most cele-brated Christian holiday. But, if they're home grown and zealot, say environmentalists who are opposed to nuclear power on principal, they might simply want to take advantage of the winter weather to sneak in."

"If they're *environmentalists*," Haskins pointed out, "then they're not looking to do any real damage."

"Right. These far out groups are happy to stage mock attacks just to point out the vulnerabilities of nuclear power, hoping to get nuc plants shut down all over the world."

"The fools don't think about the havoc they create. Or that they could actually get killed themselves in their staged drama." Haskins stared straight ahead, his jaw tight. "Or that if they're successful, a bevy of copycat attacks could be staged all over the world.

"The problem is, one of those attacks could be real then everyone's caught off guard as radioactive waste is released and we start seeing the consequences down the road."

Cara heard him loud and clear. "Still, I vote for environmentalists as the best case scenario. They don't generally deal in bombs and rocket propelled grenades."

"True that. But, let's say it is jihadists," Haskins hypothesized. "Al-Qaeda. ISIS. And they want to blow the plant. If they want to do the most damage we're not exactly looking at a highly populated area. There are other nuc plants near much more densely populated cities."

"Actually, they *could* do a lot of damage here. Think of Palo as the hub in a wheel connecting Chicago, Twin Cities, Omaha, St. Louis, and Kansas City and you've got plenty of population. The Mississippi is also a stone's throw from the plant. There would be major devastation all the way down to the Gulf if the river is contaminated with nuclear waste."

"Guess I need to brush up on my geography. Hadn't realized where we are now in relation to Chicago, et al." He slowed down for a semi when it joined traffic from an on ramp. "How much farther to Palo?"

"Not far. But this cell – and we'll call it a cell for expediency sake from now on - is not based in Palo. Per Intel, the IP address is from a computer in an apartment on the north side of Cedar Rapids."

"Why not in Palo?" Haskins glanced sideways at her.

"Because Palo is barely a town. It tops out at around a thousand people. There'd be no place to hide there without sticking out like an elephant in a strawberry patch.

"So, no. Cedar Rapids is about nine miles from the plant and close enough for a base of operation. Again, if there is an operation. And we're going to proceed as though there is."

"Do we have a head count? Any ID? Pictures? Names? Faces of these suspected cell members?"

She shook her head. "I wish."

"So we've got nothing, is what you're saying?"

"Pretty much."

"And yet they're thinking home grown – whether we're talking Jihad or environmental terror?"

She shrugged. "Only because there've been no links or threads to any known groups from the Middle East or parts unknown to this area. Facial recognition software at major airports would have spotted any ringers entering the country and headed this way and they've tagged nothing."

He pushed out a grunt. "You're forgetting that we've got a porous southern and northern border that pretty much ensures terrorists could enter with a ridiculous amount of ease."

"True, but the chatter has been pinpointed coming only from this apartment with only local contacts, which indicates they're confined to Cedar Rapids.

"While we're here," Cara continued, "both NSA and RRA are all over social media trying to find and connect more dots. We'll hear from them with details if they find a suspect. And any partial Intel we gather – names, photos – we can feed to them and they'll run it through the systems, see what they find."

"Could be a long established sleeper cell as well," he said after giving it more thought. "Planted by some offshoot of Al-

Queda or ISIS just waiting for the right place, right time to pull the trigger."

Before she could comment, a weather warning buzzed in on Cara's phone.

"Perfect," she said after opening up the bulletin then reading it out loud for Haskins' benefit.

"A southern boy like you is going to love this. National Weather Service just issued a blizzard watch. A huge storm could approach central through northeast Iowa within the next twenty-four hours. Heavy snowfall with accumulations of twelve to twenty-four inches of blowing and drifting snow and subzero windchill factors. Underlying ice will make road travel difficult to impossible."

"Sounds positively chilling."

She glanced across the front seat at him. "I guess a watch is better than a warning. Let's hope the weatherman's wrong or that we can stay ahead of this storm. Otherwise, it looks like we might be up for mission impossible."

Haskins braked lightly as a vehicle ahead of them skidded sideways on a patch of ice before the driver regained control.

"Not yet we aren't," he said on a deep breath. "We've got to get where we're going first before we've even got a mission – impossible or not."

CHAPTER TWO

"I'D SAY congratulations are in order that we made it this far." Haskins cupped a steaming mug of coffee between his big rough hands. "But I'm not in a particularly celebratory mood."

Cara grinned across the booth at him. She got it. After almost plowing the SUV into a parked car then wading through ankle deep snow in sneakers to get a room at a motel across the street from their target's apartment building, she wasn't exactly up for celebrating their safe arrival at their motel either.

Boston got snow. She was used to winter weather. She was not, however, equipped to deal with what the weather alerts were predicting. It seemed that more and more the consensus was that winter storm Holly, was coming their way. And Holly wasn't your run of the mill winter snow storm. Holly was a brute and a bully and she brought with her sub zero wind chills, deep snow and ice.

Under normal circumstances, it was going to be tricky to carry out a recon mission on possibly wannabe terrorists – who, themselves, were probably hunkered down in their digs to wait out the storm like everyone else in this part of the state.

So far a respectable four to six inches of snow covered the ground. Nothing they couldn't handle. The wind was strong but not blizzard strength. Situation manageable. Maybe they'd get lucky and the worst of it would blow itself out before it reached Cedar Rapids.

Right now they sat across from each other in a corner booth at a local pizza place waiting for their lunch/dinner to arrive. Neither had eaten since breakfast and since they had to refuel anyway and because they'd spotted this pizza place that sat kitty-corners from their recon target's rented apartment, pizza provided the perfect foil and vantage point for a little 'eyes on' recon.

Or it would have if the cold hadn't painted a coat of ice on the inside of the plate glass window beside their booth. So much for observing their target's apartment from here.

"I hope the IFR cameras are capturing more than we are." Haskins used the heel of his hand to attempt to melt a circular hole in the thin coat of ice covering the window.

As soon as they'd booked and settled into a second floor room with a direct view of the apartment building, they'd assembled their surveillance equipment and set up cameras – video, still, and infrared - in the window, aimed directly at their target site. Then they'd set out on foot to get the lay of the land and found this place.

"Yeah. Let's hope. We were lucky we got that room," Cara added as a weatherman on a big screen TV behind the bar pointed to graphs and charts and radar, foreshadowing the storm that was marching toward them. She didn't have to hear what he was saying to understand the situation.

This was now gearing up to be the biggest winter storm to hit the Midwest in almost a century. It had been rapidly working its way south and east from Canada, through the

Rockies and the plain states before dumping havoc on Minnesota where it had temporarily stalled. Now Iowa – which was originally supposed to have escaped it – could soon be smack in the middle of an icy vortex that would give the state a one two punch that was certain to, if not slow up their mission, stall it to a stand still.

Cara drew her mind away from all the potential limits the weather could place on their recon operation when the stoop-shouldered kid who'd taken their order at the counter brought their pizza with a mumbled apology for the delay.

"On your own today?" Cara smiled, feeling kind of sorry for him. He was a little older than she'd first thought – maybe twenty something. And he didn't look very happy to be here.

"Because of the weather," he said, not meeting her eyes. "Doesn't seem so bad out there yet. Seems like someone else could have come in to help out. But, as usual, they shoved it all on me."

Cara glanced at Haskins who ignored the kid's unprofessional complaining and helped himself to a slice of pizza.

"So you know, my manager called and told me to close up early. I'll be heading out in less than an hour. Not going to sit this one out by myself. I'll get you a to-go box for the pizza if you're not finished by then. No rush though," he added as an afterthought and a halfhearted attempt at sounding sorry for the inconvenience.

"That's fine," Cara said. "It's not as if we're traveling anywhere tomorrow. Sounds like this is stacking up to be a bad one."

"Yeah," he said. "You're as stuck here as I am."

Cara exchanged another look with Haskins. It was impossible not to notice how disgruntled the kid sounded.

"How'd you guys get so lucky? To get stuck here, I mean?"

Apparently he'd sized them up and decided they weren't

locals. In a neighborhood this size it made sense that he'd know or at least recognize most of his customers.

"Our flight got rerouted because of the storm in Minnesota," Haskins lied easily. "We were headed to Oregon."

"That's bad luck," he said but managed to make it sound like '*well, boohoo you. Fancy trip to Oregon got canceled. Isn't that too bad?*'

He was a kid with a chip on his shoulder all right. He needed some customer service training and a lesson in empathy because he could clearly give a hoot about their situation.

According to the plastic placard clipped to his shirt pocket, his name was Brad Carson, Jr. assist. mgr. Almost as if he suddenly thought he should show interest, Brad stopped and said, "There's a motel down the block if you need some-place to stay."

"You mean, *the* motel?" Cara laughed. One horse, one stop light, one motel neighborhood. "Yes. We got a room. We'll be all right. We'll make an adventure out of it if the forecast proves true and our flight is still canceled tomorrow."

Sensing an opening to escape any more small talk, Brad laid their ticket on the scarred wooden table top. "Let me know if you need that to-go box."

Cara watched him shuffle dejectedly back to the kitchen and shook her head. "Can we say dissatisfied lower management?"

"We could also say rude and needs a haircut and sham-poo," Haskins said dryly.

"That, too," she agreed then opened up her tablet and pulled up the Google earth map of the area while White Christmas played in the background and the furnace fan rustled the tinsel garland draped above all the windows.

An artificial tree that had seen better days, leaned in a

corner near the salad bar, its multicolored lights blinking on and off. Somewhere, someone must have hung an evergreen scented air freshener. She tried to ignore the cloying scent.

And the weather.

"Given my faith in meteorologists, I'm still holding out hope that they're overplaying their hand and blowing things out of proportion," she told Haskins. "This snow could peter out before midnight or by morning. That's the way it works sometimes."

"And if it doesn't? Peter out, as you put it?" Haskins sounded amused and not at all expecting an answer. They both knew what they were in for if the forecast was accurate.

The storm became a major complication for their mission to observe and gather Intel on their suspected homegrown terrorist cell – be it environmental or jihadist.

The hastily thrown together operation already had Cara edgy. The skimpy Intel on the suspected terrorists was little help. They didn't know if they were dealing with bomb making, AK-47 wielding, elite warriors, or pimple faced kids projecting their fantasies of a mock attack. Add in a blizzard and they had a lot bucking up against them.

They may be boots on the ground but attempting to formulate and implement a plan to spy and gather Intel on an unknown enemy while potentially fighting blistering cold, biting wind and blinding snow – well, it was going to be tricky.

"Pizza's getting cold. You gonna eat or what?"

She glanced up to see Haskins holding a spatula filled with a loaded slice of pizza toward her.

It actually smelled amazing. Considering a low fat yogurt out of a vending machine had been her only meal today and that had been around six am, she'd eat just about anything right now. She slid her plate forward. "Might as well. Can't dance."

He pushed out a sound that could pass for a chuckle then attacked his own pizza.

"So why'd you volunteer to do this?" she asked, sprinkling Parmesan cheese on her slice.

"Like our boy, Brad," he shrugged and glanced toward the kitchen, "I was filled with the holiday spirit."

She gave him a look.

"Glutton for punishment?"

More likely. Then she wondered if *she* was the punishment. "Seriously. No family celebration you hate missing?"

He chewed thoughtfully then shook his head. "Nope."

"What? They don't celebrate Christmas in North Carolina?"

Without looking at her he switched from his coffee to the soda he'd ordered and took a swig. "Yeah. They do. Just not where I come from."

Well that was a cryptic non-answer if she'd ever heard one. Did she want to ask about specifics? Did she really want to know what had put that thousand mile stare in his eyes? What made him so silent and stoic and tough?

Yeah. Unfortunately, and unwisely, she did.

"Your RRA personnel profile leaves a lot of lines blank. I don't know much of anything about your past history," she said thoughtfully.

In some instances, she knew more than she wanted to know about the rest of her team. Long deployments. Long hours of waiting and recon tended to encourage the men to talk. To each other. To her. But not Haskins. It wasn't that he was indifferent to the team. He commiserated when appropriate. Encouraged when needed. Even offered advice if asked. But *he* never asked. Not for anything. And he never talked about family or friends or ... well, anything personal.

"Why is that?"

He glanced across the table, looking puzzled. "Why is what?"

"Why is it that I don't know anything about your personal life? I mean. I'm not prying. Or maybe I am," she corrected sheepishly. "But we've been working together for a year and a half now. I know Shepard's favorite movie, his play list, and the location of his jungle rash, for God's sake. And the things Brown shares - well, there are a lot of things that I wish I could 'un-know', you know?"

He grinned. "Have you ever known me to chat?"

"Not so much, no." She chuckled and sat back. Waited until he looked at her. "Shy?"

He grunted. "Never figured I had anything interesting to say."

"I seriously doubt that."

She knew little of his personal life but knew everything about his career. This former Special Forces Squad leader, was a decorated veteran of the Iraq and Afghanistan wars. Later, he'd signed on as a securities contract specialist back in Iraq. His men had referred to him as G.I. Josh because of his gung-ho military mentality and dedication to duty. So yes. He was bound to have a lot of interesting stories he could tell, if he chose to. He never had.

She watched him help himself to another slice of pizza. Knew she should let things be. Knew that she was, in effect, propagating a friendship. And a friendship could lead to – well, it could lead to exactly what she'd decided she needed to avoid.

She should eat her pizza and drop it. Definitely, she should initiate that other conversation she'd been so bent on starting. The one that started with, *Look. We both know there's chemistry between us.* And ending with, *And we both know we can't act on it. So since we're both adults, let's clear the air, sort it out and then move on. No harm no foul.*

Yeah. That's what she should do. Instead, she stepped straight off the cliff. "Why don't you try me?"

He eyed her quizzically.

She leaned forward again. "Let me be the judge of whether you have anything interesting to say."

He was silent for so long, she wondered if she'd pushed too hard. Did he want her to back off? Leave off with the curiosity? Mind her own business?

But then a slow smile spread across that ridiculously masculine face. "So ... we're gonna *chat*, huh?"

She grinned, knowing she should put on the skids but unable to. "Only if you want to."

Again he shrugged. "Might as well. As the lady said, can't dance."

My. Goodness. Joshua Haskins. Mr. Tight Lips of the decade, was going to lay some personal info on her?

"*Do* you dance, by the way?" she asked, deciding the best course was to keep things light.

"Not sober."

A laugh bubbled out. She very much liked the wicked sense of humor that lurked beneath all that stoicism. She also realized she'd underestimated him.

It had occurred to her before that with his striking good looks and blatant air of danger, women were probably drawn to him in droves. This new found sense of humor along with, well, the 'package' that he came wrapped in — it all made him a very appealing man. There had to be women in his life.

"And do you have a steady dance partner?" The question popped out before she could filter it.

If the subject matter bothered him, he didn't show it. His thoughts were unreadable as he met and held her eyes.

"No steady partner, no." He tilted his head and studied her face before adding, "I've got this job. And a slave driver of a boss. It more or less requires all of my energy and time. Pretty much puts the kibosh on any ... *dancing*."

Whoa. She had to look away. Knew by the heat suddenly burning her cheeks that they were flushed red with embarrassment. For sure, he wasn't talking about dancing. She wasn't *thinking* about dancing either. Unless it was the horizontal kind.

Damn. She was stronger than this. Yet her thoughts had gone immediately there. To sex. With him.

If she'd been able to control her curiosity – especially about his love life – she wouldn't have strayed to this mind set now. Still, she couldn't help but feel an unaccountable rush of relief that he wasn't in a relationship. Which was ridiculous because what he did on his own time was not her concern.

Lord. One of the reasons she'd tagged him for this mission was so that she could square things away between them, pour ice water on any notion they could act on this attraction that clearly was mutual. No doubt about that any more. Not after the look he'd just given her. He could have dodged her question, too. Instead, he'd made sure she understood he didn't have a woman in his life. Interesting.

She needed to regroup. Quickly.

"Brothers? Sisters?" she asked, steering away from more trouble.

She could feel his gaze, steady on her face, as she concentrated on her pizza.

"One of each," he said finally. "Big brother. Younger sister. She's got a great kid."

Relieved that he'd rolled with the change of topic, Cara finally met his eyes. "So you keep in touch?"

After a lingering look, he nodded. "We try to. It's a little difficult given what I do, and considering Beau's in California and Jenn's in Florida. But, yeah. We keep in touch."

"Your parents?"

He chewed thoughtfully then swallowed. "No clue. Haven't had contact with either of them in years. Neither was what you'd call a contender for 'parent of the year'."

She saw pain - heavily concealed by a layer of indifference - but it was there. He felt it deep. Clearly, this was another subject she should shy away from, she thought, reminding herself again that her point in bringing him along on this op was to establish barriers not break them down.

"So what did you do for fun in your formative years?" She quickly changed the subject.

"My formative years?" The term must have amused him because he smiled. "Mostly, I got into trouble. Shot out street lights. Drive bys with baseball bats to knock mail boxes off their posts. Practiced shooting patterns in stop signs."

"All federal offenses," she pointed out but didn't attach any guilt. Instead she saw a t-shirt wearing, BB gun toting, cocky kid causing mischief. A kid who had grown into a man who could accept who he was and where he'd come from and had risen above it despite his parents' neglect.

"Yes, ma'am. Are you going to cuff me?"

He was flirting. And it was totally working.

"So *rural* North Carolina," she said so quickly that it made him grin. "And a rebellious, misspent youth."

He flashed a full on smile this time. "I thought I was pretty tough shit."

"Sounds like you were."

He considered his pizza then took another long pull on his soda. "Pretty much, yeah. Partly because I was ornery as sin. And partly because I had to be. We all did. The economy was crap back then. The old man went where he could to find work then drank away his paycheck at the local watering hole. Mom ... well, she wasn't in the picture much either. You can probably fill in the blanks."

No self pity. Just matter of fact. *We all did.* He seemed to have overcome it well. "Sounds rough. But it doesn't seem to have scarred you overmuch."

He pushed out an amused laugh. "Not over much. No."

Unable to help herself, she smiled with him, curious. "Why is that funny?"

"Because there are a lot of people who would strongly disagree."

"That you're not scarred?"

"Oh, yeah. Speaking of scarring." He gave her a considering look. "What about you? Any damage to speak of on the road to who you are?"

Not scarred, but skillful – at least at diverting the conversation away from himself when he wanted to.

Considering she'd already learned more about him in the last five minutes than she had in the last eighteen months, she backed off and lifted her slice of pizza. "You probably already have me figured out."

"Probably," he agreed.

That made her laugh. And it made her nervous. "I'll undoubtedly regret it, but let's hear it. What have you figured out about me?"

He cocked a brow, wary.

"Off the record," she assured him. "No fear of reprisal from your CO. Go ahead. Let me have it."

"Okay. But remember - you wanted to hear this."

Then he drew a deep breath and reluctantly let fly.

"You come from a fairly privileged, upper middle class family. Raised with values. Those values drove you. You *are* driven. To excel. No other option. You wouldn't give yourself one. A woman doesn't earn a leadership position in an organization as complex and powerful as RRA unless she's a ball buster. No insult intended."

Whoa! He pretty much had her nailed. Except for the ball-buster part. Anyway, she didn't think of herself that way.

She toyed with her glass. Was contemplating if she really came across as that power hungry bitch who sacrificed all for success when his voice brought her head up.

"But you're human, too," he added, compelling her to hold his very sincere gaze. "You consider others. You don't ask what can't be delivered. You're intuitive that way. It's part of what makes you a good CO."

She felt a little raw suddenly. A lot exposed. He saw all that? On their operations? Behind her uniform, her leader persona, with her hair pulled into a tight bun and her face free of make up and, she'd thought, free of expression if she was doing things right?

And today, in a heavy blue sweater and jeans, stripped of her rank, making her his equal, he apparently saw right through her. Or to the heart of her.

It was a little frightening that he was so on point. She *had* been brought up on the privileged side. She *had* been taught values that she held to this day and always would.

"Don't worry, sir," he said, falling back into their assigned roles. "Your secrets are safe with me."

She huffed out a breath. "Apparently I don't have any secrets from you."

He considered her with a thoughtful look. "That bothers you, does it?"

She shrugged. But, yeah. It bothered her. Bothered her that this man, whom she had originally pegged as a hard ass with a chip on his shoulder and a situational awareness that was confined to their missions, was much more of a thinker and more intuitive than she'd given him credit for being.

Not that she'd thought he was uninspired or unintelligent. The opposite was true. She'd thought, well, that he was one dimensional. Soldier dimensional. Mission focused dimensional. She'd pigeonholed him early on as a warrior and not much beyond that. Her very huge mistake.

As they lapsed into a silence filled with speculation, she also realized that these new dimensions to his persona actually made this physical attraction a bit more dicey.

Physical was physical. Throw in emotion, however, and yeah, things got sticky. Super glue sticky.

"You do have *one* secret," he said with a stone face that gained all of her attention.

She tried to avoid looking at him. Tried and failed when his magnetic gray eyes met hers. "And what secret is that?"

"What *did* they do to you for your initiation into RRA?"

Damn. He made her smile again. "I think I'll keep that one to myself for a while yet."

He propped his forearms on the booth top and wiped his hands on his napkin. "That bad, huh?"

A smile played around her mouth as she thought about what those guys had done to her. She hadn't smiled back then. She'd been mad as hell. Just like Haskins had been angry when he'd discovered that Anastasia was a set up. "Yup. That bad."

It was interesting that it had taken eighteen months for him to reference the Princess Anastasia fiasco, but it seemed he was curious about her RRA initiation after all.

She pushed her plate away. Full. "What about you? You still mad about the princess?"

For an answer, he gave her an inscrutable glance then motioned for Brad to bring them a to-go box.

"I'm going to go with *still mad*," she decided which made him grin.

"I don't get mad," he assured her as he boxed up the left over pizza – it might be all they had to eat the rest of the day and night. "I get–"

"Even," she said before he finished.

He stood and shoved his arms into his jacket. "Something like that."

His words sounded playful not threatening.

Yet she felt a little threatened. By the icy hot chill his expression sent skittering down her spine. By the sudden liquid heat that sluiced through her blood at the thought of what he might have in mind for getting even with her.

And he didn't have a steady dance partner.

The look in his eyes, the sexy smile in his voice, and the implied promise that he did, in fact, intend to get even, conjured all kinds of off limit scenarios to play out in her mind. Scenarios involving him and her, naked on a bed, and a very improper punishment being meted out with torturous, blissful languor.

Holy God. Heat shot through her body and nearly buckled her knees.

"Whoa." He reached out and cupped her shoulders to steady her. "You okay?"

"Fine," she said too quickly. "I guess I stood up too fast." Then she practically sprinted for the door.

CHAPTER THREE

"Just how do you propose we go about this?" Josh asked Cara as they trudged back to the 'seen better days' motel with their newly purchased winter gear.

When he'd paid their bill, Josh had asked Brad where they could buy some heavier clothes. He'd told them about a Ma and Pa sporting goods store slash gun shop just around the corner. As soon as they'd left the restaurant, they'd hit the store.

A hobbled up senior with a bald head, a fit frame, and a Tom Selleck mustache was about to hang the closed sign on the door as they walked in.

"Caught me just in time," he said with a smile. "Come on in. I just figured everybody was hunkered down to wait out the storm. You take your time.

"Jack Halpert," he'd added, extending his hand. "You don't see what you want, give me a yell. I've probably got it in the back room."

He'd been right about that. If Jack didn't have it, you didn't need it. Jeans, flannel shirts, snowmobile suits, insulated underwear, fishing gear, long guns, pistols, and ammo –

Jack was inventoried to the gills with every kind of sports wear and equipment imaginable.

"And a very Merry Christmas to you both," Jack had said with a wide grin as he'd closed the door and locked up behind them forty-five minutes later.

They were loaded up with boots, gloves, caps, jackets and enough hand warmers to keep their fingers warm for a decade. Add in the left over pizza to ward off hunger, they were set for the rest of a long night of surveillance.

"I have a feeling we just made a very Merry Christmas for the Halperts," Cara said, wrestling with packages as they walked on slippery sidewalks.

"And did you get a load of that tidy little arsenal behind his gun counter?" Josh had been surprised. Who knew they'd find weaponry like that in something other than a huge franchise store. Halpert knew his stuff. "Might come in handy if we have a need for some firepower."

They hadn't brought weapons with them and Josh knew that Cara must feel as naked as he did without at least a side piece. Weapons would have brought unwanted attention at the airports and besides, Cara reminded him now, "Recon. This is all about recon, not confrontation with weapons."

"Which brings us back to, do we have a plan yet?"

"I don't know," Cara said, fumbling for her key as they reached their second floor room via the outside stairway and balcony. "Do we? I know you weren't just chewing on pizza. You've been chewing on the problem."

"I have," Josh said, finding his key first and inserting it into the motel room door. He shoved it open and let Cara enter first as the wind blew snow and cold in behind them. "Let's talk."

"Wow. Another chat. I might get to thinking the dam broke." Cara grinned as she unwound her scarf, unzipped her jacket and tossed both, along with her packages, on a chair.

"Talking strategy is not chatting."

"If it makes you feel better to think so."

She smiled at him again. A soft, knowing, 'I've got your number' smile that did not prompt Josh to salute. Or to react in any way that was appropriate for a subordinate to react to his CO.

Something had happened since they'd landed and eaten and 'chatted'. Something Josh had managed to avoid at all costs since he'd discovered that she was his CO and it was Anastasia he was still pissed at and not Cara.

Anastasia had been a royal pain. Cara, on the other hand, was a professional. He admired her expertise, her skill set, her bravery, her leadership qualities and her interaction with the team. As long as he kept her in the 'superior to subordinate' box, all was well. Only when he let his guard down and started observing her as a woman did he get in trouble.

He didn't let that happen often. Sometimes, however, it was unavoidable. Zero dark thirty on a hot, sultry Indonesian night, the two of them taking their turns at watch in the steamy jungle while the rest of the team caught power naps. The close call when an ISIS militant broke through their defenses in Syria and had a whack at her with his machete. She'd handled the terrorist in short order but when Josh had seen her in such close contact danger, then seen blood ooze from the slash in her bare arm, he'd felt not only a dark fear but a concern that far exceeded anxiety for a combat buddy or his CO.

He'd scrambled to her side before he'd realized he'd even moved from his position. And until the team medic had stitched her up, shot her full of antibiotics, field dressed her arm, and pronounced her good to go, he hadn't taken his eyes off of her or drawn a steady breath.

Those were the times it was the most difficult to avoid that she had become more to him than his CO.

She was a woman. A gorgeous woman. That she was capable and competent and intelligent and outranked him might have turned some men off. Not him. It only made her more appealing. Seeing her in the deep jungle, sweat making her camos cling to her curves, her hair escaping from her no nonsense bun, and face black covering her cheeks to camouflage her in the dark should have made her less appealing. But the core strength beneath all those soft curves was a turn on like he'd never experienced.

That's when his inner strength and determination came into play. That's when he employed self-control in spades. He could skate by showing concern for a fellow team member, but anything more crossed a line.

Superior. Subordinate. That's where it needed to stop and end with the two of them. That's where it had to stop. He'd made damn sure of it.

But now – now they'd 'chatted'. Over pizza for God's sake. With her beautiful blond hair tumbling down over her shoulders. Her soft blue sweater emphasizing her generous breasts. Her worn jeans fitting her like they'd been painted on. She looked feminine and approachable. And so sexy he'd had to bite his tongue to keep from telling her so.

He'd flirted with her. He'd actually flirted with his CO. Instead of stripping the hide off of his back, she'd smiled. She'd even laughed and damned if that guard he so religiously kept up when it came to her hadn't crumbled.

Do you have a steady dance partner?

Lord, help him. Talk about a game changer. The fact that she'd asked, the fact that she'd cared then looked both embarrassed and relieved when he'd said *no, no steady partner* – well, hell. If he'd had any question that she was as attracted to him as he was to her before, he had his answer now.

Now here they were. Alone in a motel room in a snow storm. And he had 'dancing' on his mind.

Couldn't happen.

This was work. This was a clutch, albeit reconnaissance only assignment. And he needed to keep his head in the game.

Knowing that she might want to 'dance' with him as much as he wanted to 'dance' with her, however ...well. It made him edgy as hell.

"You ready to review some of this footage?" Her voice snapped him back to the moment as she wirelessly linked up her laptop to the surveillance equipment.

"Yeah. Sure. But start without me." He grabbed the ice bucket. "Be right back."

He caught a glimpse of her face as he flew to the door. She looked a little perplexed at his abrupt escape but didn't question his sudden need for ice in the middle of a snow storm with the temperature hovering around twenty degrees Fahrenheit.

"Better put your jacket on," she called after him.

"I'm fine."

"If you say so. I'll go ahead and start checking the feeds," she said as he closed the door behind him.

Then he leaned back against it, clutching the ice bucket to his chest as the snow hit him in the face and accumulated at his feet on the outside balcony.

"Get a freaking grip, Haskins," he muttered and headed down the slippery walkway toward the ice machine.

Cripes, he hoped she hadn't sensed how badly he'd needed to escape from the room.

From her.

From *them*.

And their damn 'chats'.

He was way out of line and uneasy as hell with his reaction to this side of Cara Graves. She was softer. More approachable. Even vulnerable if the look on her face when he'd categorized her as a ball-buster was any indication.

It had bothered her. A lot of women in power would have been proud of that designation. He hadn't seen pride in her eyes, though. He'd seen disappointment. A suggestion that while she owned everything else he'd said, she didn't particularly welcome that hard core assessment. That reaction made her even more human.

He'd also seen hurt. The biggest surprise of all from this tough as nails commanding officer who faced down terrorists for a living and wasn't afraid to chew a little ass if one of her team – all of whom out weighed her by a good eighty pounds - fell out of line.

"And that, Wingnut, is what you have to remember," he reminded himself aloud, headed for the ice machine and started filling the bucket while he stood like a dweeb and shivered in the icy wind. Cara Graves was his CO. They were on a mission.

He made himself regroup. Think about what, if anything, they might find on the surveillance tapes. Hopefully something they could latch on to and get this mission accomplished and head back to HQ. Thank God they'd be busy reviewing the feed for the next several hours.

As soon as they'd checked in and gotten settled into their second floor room, they'd set up the equipment in the window, training it on the apartment building and the entrance to their suspect's exterior apartment door, which was on the second floor with an outside stairway.

Josh didn't hold out much hope of capturing any clear images given the falling snow and wind obscuring the view, but the infrared equipment might pick up heat signatures and give them an idea of how many cell members were currently inside – if they were, in fact, a terrorist cell. He was eager, on that count, to get back to the room and see if the new IFR camera worked as advertised.

Like the NVG's equipped with IFR and a viewing screen worn on the wrist, they were field testing a new stationary IFR camera. These cameras, unlike their predecessors, had the capacity to detect heat signatures through glass, concrete and wooden walls. True that left out steel, but this was a huge improvement and would give them a great advantage. If they worked.

With his bucket full of ice and feeling half frozen, he was about to head back to the room when he spotted a row of vending machines. Cara – make that Lt. Graves – had a sweet tooth. Chocolate was her favorite. And before he pitted the wisdom of treating her against the notion that the gesture was far too personal, he'd unloaded most of his pocket change into the machines.

Then he stood there in the cold a while longer, debating whether he should throw away the chocolate or take it back to her. Good, God. What? Was he fourteen? He was stalling. He knew that. And he'd have stalled longer if he wasn't half frozen to death.

On a shivering breath, he finally turned back toward their room, but stopped abruptly when he caught sight of a man walking toward the apartment building they had under surveillance.

He waited, wanting to see where he was headed. Josh was a good twenty yards away from the building but he backed into the shadows of the overhang, just in case he could be spotted. He brushed the accumulated snow away from his face, not sure he trusted what he thought he was seeing.

A little after 5:00 pm in December in the Midwest, it was already pitch dark. Couple that with the falling snow and the wind whipping it around, visibility was horrible. Still ... he swore he recognized the man who climbed the apartment steps then rapped on the door.

CARA SAT on one of the queen-sized beds, her tablet propped on her crossed legs, reviewing the camera's surveillance feed when Haskins burst inside the room. A gust of frigid air and a heavy dusting of snow swept in with him.

She shivered. "Well, if it isn't Jack Frost."

The tips of his nose and ears were red from the cold and as soon as he set the ice bucket on the table by the door and tossed a glorious assortment of chocolate candies and bars on the bed, he started blowing on his hands to warm them up.

"Oh. My. God. You read my mind." She snatched up a Snickers and ripped open the wrapper. "I do my best work fueled on chocolate."

Of course, he knew that. She often brought a stash with her on their ops. No doubt, he'd seen her peel many a wrapper off a half-melted chocolate bar in the jungle. The guys teased her about her sweet tooth. Well, most of the guys. Haskins didn't tease about anything.

"Guess what I just saw," he said and poured himself a glass of water.

She glanced up at him. "A miniature sleigh eight tiny reindeer?"

His expression was grim. "Picture greasy headed kid making pizza."

She pinched her brows together. "Brad?"

"Brad."

"Okay. So why is that noteworthy? He said he was closing up and going home soon after we left."

"Yeah, he did. What's noteworthy, is where he went."

He looked far too grave. When it finally hit her, she understood why. "Seriously?"

"Yup. Just walked up the stairs and went inside the apartment. Should show up on the surveillance feed soon."

She frowned. Blinked. "Holy hell."

"And then some."

"Maybe he was delivering a pizza on his way home," she suggested, still confounded by this piece of news.

"And maybe Elvis is alive and hiding in the fridge next to the left over pizza."

She set her laptop aside and walked to the window. Arms crossed under her breasts, she stared toward the apartment as if wishing it so, could make her see inside. "I'd say he didn't seem like the type if we didn't both know that there is no exact 'type'."

"Disgruntled low level employee, not living the American dream? Disenfranchised with his life or lack of it? I'd say he's the prototype for the profile."

Quickly returning to the bed, she grabbed her phone and wrote an encrypted message to her RRA stateside contact.

'Mission critical request: Person of interest: Brad Carson. Caucasian. Brn hair and eyes. Approx. 5'10". age:18 – 25. 160-170#. Jr Asst Mger of Taste of Italy pizza restaurant, E 88th St. Cedar Rapids, IA. Suspected cell member. Send all discovered Intel ASAP.'

She showed the message to Haskins for his approval or additions and when he nodded, hit send.

"I didn't sense any undue interest or any suspicion about us on his part," she said aloud, then glanced up at Haskins who was busy rechecking the positions of the surveillance cameras.

"Agreed." He turned back to her when he was satisfied with the set up. "He just wanted us out of there so he could leave. But on the off chance he did suspect us, I reckon the poison he laced into the pizza will be kicking in very soon now."

Because he was being intentionally ridiculous, one corner of her mouth turned up. "Ha Ha. And reckon? That a North Carolina word?"

"I reckon it is."

She was in full recon mode now and didn't hesitate to pat the bed beside her. "Come and see what we've filmed so far."

He took a long step toward her, hesitated, then sat down close enough to see her monitor but not too close to her. "Anything but snow?"

"Plenty of that but until you saw Brad the Terrorist – still can't wrap my head around that – it doesn't appear that anyone came or went."

"What about the IFR?"

"That's what I want to show you. Hold on. Let me pull up the footage. There." She clicked in coding, waited, then pointed to the center of the monitor. "It's brilliant! Works just like R&D said it would."

"I'll be damned. That's stellar."

"Yeah," she agreed, grinning. "Absolutely stellar.

"So far I'm only seeing one heat signature."

He leaned in closer ... and she froze, hyper-aware of being surrounded by his scent. Something masculine and clean with the underlying crispness of winter. Even more, where a moment ago, she'd been all business, she suddenly felt enmeshed in his presence as the mattress dipped and his shoulder pressed hers, warm and strong and oh, my, God, this was horrible.

Against all determination not to be, she couldn't shake the feeling of being overwhelmed by not only his proximity but by his size and the strength that came with it. And ... talk about heat signatures.

"That's all I see, too. Should be two once Brad shows up

in the footage," he suggested as he studied the images, mercifully oblivious to her reaction.

Or so she thought until he glanced sideways at her, swallowed hard then quickly looked away.

She had to concentrate to hear her own thoughts above her pounding heart. "The apartment's small. Walls can't be that thick so I don't think we're missing anyone. Close quarters makes for lack of definition in the imagery if they're clustered together."

His attention was focused laser-like on the fuzzy red image that sometimes moved, sometimes stayed stationary but pretty much always stuck in the same general area of the apartment – like he was huddling over a table – checking details and plans? "How much video have you had a chance to review?" His voice had grown rusty.

She drew a steadying breath. "About five minutes' worth. That's how long you were gone."

It was becoming more and more difficult to focus on the infrared footage as he shifted his weight again for a better look at the screen. Now their hips also connected; the length of his thigh pressed against hers.

Heart thundering wildly, unable to resist the temptation, she turned her head to look up at him. At his ruggedly handsome profile, at the scar on his chin that he'd gotten in the Philippines, at the jump of his pulse beating heavily in his neck.

For a suspended moment she couldn't breathe. Couldn't move. Neither, apparently, could he. But then he slowly turned his head and gazed down at her.

Their eyes locked, his liquid and molten and so intense, her breath caught. And her heart went even wilder.

CHAPTER FOUR

THE SLIGHTEST ADJUSTMENT, the most minuscule realignment of their heads, and their mouths would touch.

Cara wanted it to happen. Wanted it more than anything she ever remembered wanting. For too long she'd wondered what he tasted like. Too often, she'd longed to feel the pressure of his lips against hers, the thrust of his tongue into her mouth. The weight of his big body over hers.

Knowing it shouldn't happen, knowing nothing good could come of it, she still indulged in the need. Couldn't help herself and leaned closer until the warmth of his breath touched her lips.

"Cara," he whispered, brushing his lips lightly over hers for a long, beautiful moment ... before a sudden rush of cold and disappointment replaced them.

He stood abruptly. Walked back to the surveillance IFR camera. "Is there ... any fine tuning that can be done to these?" His voice sounded gruff as he bent over the camera and checked the shutter speed.

For a moment, she sat there. Frozen in place. She couldn't decide if she felt more relief than disappointment that he'd had the good sense to back away. To avert a breach of RRA protocol and a professional mistake of epic proportions.

"Um … let me see." It amazed her that her voice wasn't trembling. "There might be a couple of minor adjustments I can make."

He gave her plenty of room as she walked to the camera, leaned over and with shaking hands, rechecked the settings. "I don't know if that will help with clarity or not."

She stood up straight, adjusted her sweater. She had to get a hold of this. And she had to do it now.

Before she could change her mind, she drew a steadying breath then turned and faced him. "Look. Um. We need to talk. About …" she gestured toward the bed. "About what almost happened just now."

Haskins turned to the window, stared outside. "I'd say we've talked enough."

Then he swung around and glared at her, tucked his fingers into the front pocket of his jeans and leaned a shoulder against the wall. "Talking's what started this …" It was his turn to lift a hand and gesture toward the bed, "… lapse in judgment."

She closed her eyes, nodded, trying not to be hurt by his anger. "True. But we both know that we've had this … this attraction between us long before today."

He looked at the floor. Looked at the cameras. Anywhere but at her. "That's a fact."

"Here's another fact," she said, finally getting herself together and realigning her priorities. "We can't act on it."

Silence settled, heavy and thick and as cold as the winter night before he spoke. "Agreed."

She heard as much determination as reluctance in that one word. Just as much as she felt.

He met her eyes. "So why did you bring me along? You had to know this could become a problem."

"I did. Yes. But I decided it was time to face it. Get things out in the open and make sure we're both squared away with what can and can't happen between us."

His eyes turned dark and distant. "Right. Yeah. All right. Consider things squared away. The operative word is nothing. Nothing can happen."

She felt another moment of regret. "Look. I'm not telling you anything you don't know, but RRA has a no fraternization policy. Anything between us – even if it's just physical – is off limits."

In an instant, his expression shifted from fatalistic acceptance to a much more intense emotion. "Even if it's just physical," he repeated, and again, the bitterness in his tone shocked her. "Got it. Don't worry, *sir*," he said crisply. "Situation normal from this point forward."

"Haskins," she said, more softly when he held her gaze. She needed him to know, suddenly, that if it weren't for their careers, things would have been different. "You have to realize that I care about you. Different circumstances, different–"

"Priorities," he supplied for her. "Different priorities."

The words stung with accusation. Like he was reminding her that she had a choice. That they both did.

"I've got it." He worked his jaw. "We can't ... but might have if there weren't more important factors to consider."

Oh, yeah. He was angry.

"No need to 'chat' about it," he added before she could process all of the emotions she was feeling. "We're not kids. And we've got a job to do."

Then he grabbed his back pack, walked to the bathroom and shut the door behind him. Through the thin walls, she heard the shower go on full blast.

For a long time, she stood there, arms crossed beneath her breasts, shivering, but not from the cold. From his rage.

And from an encroaching realization that before tonight she had never once considered that she could lose so much more by following the rules than she could by breaking them.

JOSH STRIPPED and stepped into the steaming spray. Disgust didn't begin to cover what he felt with himself. He still wasn't sure what had given him the gumption to pull away from a kiss that would have led to irreversible trouble.

Trouble and sex. Hot, amazing, steamy sex with a woman he'd fantasized about for months. In the tropical jungle. In the belly of a transport bird flying home from a mission. In his narrow bunk, at night, when sleep wouldn't come and images of her face and hair and body wouldn't go away.

He'd been so close! Just now. On that bed. Close to heaven. Closer to hell if he'd ruined his career and hers along with it with one irresponsible action.

Even if it was just physical.

He still wasn't sure why her throw-away words ticked him off. It wasn't as if he'd been thinking long term. Or thinking with his head for that matter. Hell, he didn't know what he'd been thinking – except how incredible she would feel, naked beneath him. He'd been thinking how he'd never wanted another woman the way he wanted her. Thinking that maybe, finally, he'd found that piece of himself that had always been missing.

Which was ridiculous. There was nothing missing. He was a loner. Always had been. Didn't expect to change now.

He twisted off the faucets and grabbed a towel from the bar, then dragged the rough, worn cotton over his body. Rationalized: She was a woman. He was a man. They were attracted to each other. Didn't mean they had to act on it.

And it especially didn't mean that he had to be thinking happily ever after.

And where had that even come from?

He loved his career. *Lived* his career. Getting accepted into RRA had been the hill he'd been willing to die on, just to be a part of the organization. He'd finally made it. His hard work had paid off.

He'd proven to himself and others that he was more than what he'd come from. Much more than that tossed-aside kid who'd done his damnedest to ruin his life before he'd finally gotten wise and turned himself around. And he wasn't willing to throw it all away now. Or to take her down with him.

He'd been a fool to let her get so close him this afternoon. To let the paradigm shift between them from a work relationship to something more.

More intimate. More familiar. More heated.

Well, no more. She'd laid it on the line. And she was right. Done and done. All he had to do was think about the crap she'd put him through as Anastasia and he'd get angry all over again. Blend Cara and the Princess and he should get his head back on straight.

Except, he realized, as he dragged the towel over his wet hair, even at her worst, Anastasia had flipped his switch, too.

But he was also a soldier. He had a job to do. That's why he'd managed to force himself away from a kiss they had both wanted and would have led to more problems than he'd ever have time to solve.

He wiped the steam away from the mirror. "As soon as you wrap up this operation, buddy, you're putting in for a transfer out of her unit."

A post half a continent away from her ought to do it. He'd be away from temptation. Away from the one woman he'd ever truly wanted and the foolish notion that somehow he could have her.

He was so screwed.

———

"ARE YOU READY?"

Avoiding Haskins' eyes, Cara looked him up and down to make certain he was covered from head to toe in white. White jacket, pants, gloves, white face mask ... even white boots.

It might have been excessive but what, on this operation, hadn't been? They both looked like ads for chic white snow gear – something the rich and famous might wear for the ski season at Aspen or Vail. One thing about Halpert, his merchandise didn't lack for design or style.

On a more practical note, however, since the snow had picked up again in weight and velocity, they were sure to be practically invisible against the backdrop of a literally white Christmas. They'd been on scene for close to four hours now and had done as much long distance surveillance as they could. They were going to have to get up close and personal.

Thanks to NSA's access of information, from blueprints to logistical documents, they knew everything they needed to know about the apartment building's layout and access points. What they didn't know was who, besides Brad the pizza man, was in that apartment. She hadn't heard any response to her text request yet.

In the meantime, she wanted to plant a bug so they could also listen in. Haskins looked ready. Apparently there were a lot of winter hunters in this part of the world because Halpert's store had been stocked to the gills with white winter wear.

"You clear on the plan?" Cara asked him.

He nodded, fiddling with his gloves. "One sneak and peek coming up."

Besides concentrating on keeping things strictly business, they'd spent the last hour pitting pass/fail tactics against each other for what could make or break the success of their mission. After discussing and tossing aside several options they'd finally decided to go for broke with a sneak and peek and hope they'd get a better handle on what and who they were up against.

Haskins, like her, had flipped a switch and transitioned back into warrior mode. If he was still thinking about their mutual problem, he didn't show it. Wouldn't show it nor would he let it affect their mission.

Neither, would she.

It was all business now.

Her phone vibrated just as they were about to go out the door.

"Hold on." She fished it out of a pocket, pulled a glove off with her teeth and pulled up the message. "It's Intel on our pizza man.

"Brad Carson is local," she read aloud. "High school drop out. Loner. Parents divorced. Still lives with his mother. Limited social media activity. Mostly a gamer until he hooked up with an Andrew Peet online three years ago."

"I take it we're heading for Peet's apartment?"

"Yup. They've sent Intel on Peet, too," she added. "He's another local. Another loser. Older than Carson. Late twenties, string of entry level jobs that never panned out. At the time he and Brad hooked up, Peet had a somewhat radical but low profile on social media."

"Jihadist?" Haskins speculated as he rechecked his gear.

She shook her head. "Environmentalist. Big beef with nuclear energy."

"Bingo. Now this is making sense. How convenient that they both live near the Palo plant. That's almost too easy."

"So it would seem." She scanned the information. "The

report says that after their cyber friendship developed, Brad's social media footprint gradually became heavy with environmental propaganda – mostly espousing the nuclear energy field, like his new mentor, Peet. But about two years ago, they both went silent."

"Until NSA found that little nugget of chatter last week."

She nodded. "Since we provided them with Brad's basics earlier, they've been able to link the two up again and found very recent references to environmental manifestos on the dark web, targeting the nuclear power plants in operation in the US. The manifestos were written by anonymous authors but the source document's IP address lands here."

"Enter who we now know are Brad Carson and Andrew Peet. Surprised NSA didn't move on them two years ago when they first started making noise. Put the fear of God and the FBI into their screwed up little souls."

She'd thought about that, too. "Difficult to move in when they hadn't done anything. Ever. Then, when they disappeared a couple of years ago, it was easy to speculate that they fizzled out."

"So NSA hasn't even been monitoring them?"

"No reason after they dropped off the radar. You know how that goes. Misfits and outcasts get together, find a common cause, beat on their chests about righting wrongs, vow to show, with a mock attack, how Armageddon is a mistake away and, whoops ... one of them gets mad and splits. Or one of them finds a girlfriend or religion – or God forbid, one of them gets a real job - and their 'cause' loses momentum and ends up dissolving."

Haskins double checked that his jacket was zipped. "Which is why we're still not sure if this is the real thing or a wannabe freedom fighter's dream resurrected."

"Unfortunately, yes."

"At least we've got a loose handle on these two suspected

environmental terrorists or terrorist wannabes. And we're not dealing with jihadists. Always a plus."

Thanks to her text, yeah, they did have actionable Intel now. Cara, too, felt a little better about what they were going to find. Not a hotbed of combat experienced jihadists armed to the teeth, but a motley pair of outcasts who missed the sleigh to Santa's island of misfit toys.

"Let's get this show on the road then." Haskins tugged a white stocking cap over his hair. "See if these two plan to fish or cut bait. Or if they're capable of either."

She pulled on her own cap. "No time like the present."

CHAPTER FIVE

BRAD DIDN'T WANT to go to Peet's tonight. He wanted to go home. He wanted to eat some of the chili his mom had made for him – not think about the mess his life had become.

But here he was. Wading through shin deep snow on the way to Peet's apartment. Knowing that if Trent Matthews wasn't there waiting with Peet, he'd be there soon. And with nothing good on his mind.

God, he hated Matthews. Everything in his life had changed when Matthews had joined the group six months ago. Everything.

Snow fell wet and cold on his face and dampened his hair as he trudged reluctantly down the sidewalk. The walk gave him time to think about the good old days. The days when they hadn't had to be accountable to anyone but their original group. The days before Matthews had goaded them into believing they needed to fulfill their destiny.

Destiny? They didn't have a destiny before Matthews. They'd been sincere, yes. Him and Peet. Then Gary, Chad, Max and Roger had joined them. The six of them had met in a chat room nightly for a year or so, all of them gamers, all of them also firmly united in the idea that atomic energy was dangerous as an energy source and that they should do everything in their power to show the world how dangerous it was.

They'd clicked as a group. They'd had amazing, into the middle of the night, discussions. They'd fantasized and schemed and developed a cyber exercise similar to Dungeons and Dragons and competed with each other on writing the best, most creative mock scenarios showing how ease it would be to bring down nuc plants on American soil. Since all of them lived in or near Cedar Rapids, they'd even used the Palo plant as their attack plan prototype, finding out everything they could on plant security and weaknesses.

It had been challenging, and uplifting and ... and pretend. And though they'd never said it aloud, they'd all known that there wasn't one among them who would initiate any type of attack – mock or otherwise - on an atomic plant.

Then Matthews had found a worm hole and squeezed into their secret online organization. At first ... well at first, he'd been like a new toy. He'd been a gifted strategist, a bold thinker and he'd breathed new life into a game that had lost some of its edge.

So yeah, when Peet invited Matthews to come to one of their face to face meetings to consolidate their 'virtual reality' concepts six months ago, they'd all welcomed him.

But then they'd met him in person. He was over twice their age! Too old to be playing games. It was ... weird. Uncomfortable. And it turned out, it wasn't a game to him.

Matthews soon made it known that he was up to taking action. He really wanted to stage a mock attack on the Palo plant.

"It's not as if it isn't planned out flawlessly," Matthews would reason, his dark eyes flashing like a zealot's while his unruly mop of salt and pepper hair sprang around his face. "You guys haven't missed a thing. The plan is foolproof. Infallible. Brilliant. And it's not as if you don't believe in the cause."

They'd been horrified when he talked like that. Then bewildered. Then they'd become mesmerized at his suggestion. At his belief that they could really do something important.

But worse, they'd felt shamed. Shamed when he called them out as frauds. With one look, one statement, Matthews made them realize that all these years they'd spent talking big, making grandiose plans, working through the night with grit in their eyes and freedom ringing in their ears - that they had just been playing at being important. Toying with the notion that they could do something for the greater good.

By the end of that first evening, Matthews had halfway convinced them all that to not follow through on their plan would be an abomination. It would be a failure on their part not to do, for their country, what men like Washington, and Lincoln and even JFK had done. Those men had changed the course of the nation. They'd saved lives and freedoms and restored faith and dreams.

Didn't Brad and Peet and the others want to make that kind of impact on mankind? Give humanity that gift?

Brad was shivering by the time he hit the bottom step that led up to Peet's apartment as he remembered that he hadn't been able to sleep that night after meeting Matthews. He'd had many sleepless nights since, grappling with his safe but unremarkable life, pitted against the true opportunity, as Matthews had called it, of doing something courageous and earth-shattering and, most importantly, necessary to save mankind.

The federal government, however, tended to frown on activists who went too far. He was not prepared to go to prison. His mom would be mortified.

Still, the next few times they'd met with Matthews, to a

man, they were changed. Still hesitant. Still in disbelief that Matthews actually wanted to act on a plan that until he'd shown up, had been a game. But more than anything else, Matthews continued to instill shame in them. Not by calling them cowards, but by pointing out their combined genius and making them face the fact that children played games. Men acted on their beliefs.

It had started to feel real then. Gradually, Matthews's words didn't sound so shocking. Instead they made sense. Gave them a true purpose. But the night Jeannie Pruitt dropped in to their in-person meeting with Matthews, was the night that games had turned in to reality.

Ready to get out of the cold, even if it meant confronting Matthews, Brad sighed heavily and rapped on Peet's door.

* * *

Christmas decorations swung from the top of lamp posts, shaken by the wind. Sparkling snow clung to the lights, dimming them. Neither Cara nor Josh glanced up at the bells, trees, candles, and snowflakes twinkling valiantly above them through the deluge of snow that had started falling in earnest.

They were mission focused. And the mission was to infiltrate the three story, twenty unit apartment building undetected via the maintenance door at the rear of the structure.

From there, they would access the inside stairwell, ascend to the second floor and approach apartment 25, located near the middle of the floor. At that point they would install a listening device for further monitoring. Neither Peet nor Brad would be able to detect the bug Haskins would attach above the outer door frame.

Gaining access to the building was painfully easy. There was no street traffic due to the weather. No security guard. They'd counted on the good citizens of this neighborhood to be tucked inside and riding out the storm from the comfort of their homes. They hadn't been wrong. No one in their right mind would be out on a night like this. No one but a pair of RRA operatives who were highly suspicious they were on a wild goose chase, but were intent on doing their job anyway.

They stood under the cover of a shop awning, surveying the apartment building. Then, with a nod from Haskins, they crossed the street and hugged the west side of the building. High security it was not. A surveillance camera, mounted high on the corner of the building, was covered with snow. Still, they avoided it as they approached the back door. Despite exposing his fingers to the cold, Haskins worked fast and adeptly with his pick kit.

"Got it," he whispered and pushed the door open wide enough for Cara to slip through ahead of him before he closed the door behind them.

The maintenance room at the very back of the building was standard cinder block walls covered in institutional gray paint. Inside were the electrical panels, furnace, HVAC unit and multiple plumbing lines. The neoprene soles of their boots moved soundlessly over raw concrete floors, leaving prints of melted snow in their wake that would evaporate soon after they ex-filtrated the building.

One of her father's favorite sayings came to mind. *Like a ship at sail, they'd leave no trail.*

The flashlight on Cara's phone lit the small room and showed them the hall access door. Silently, Haskins pushed it open and slipped into the first floor communal hallway lit with dim security lights.

They didn't anticipate much hall traffic, but with Cara in the lead, she checked around the corner then gave Haskins the okay to go ahead of her.

He slipped around her and opened the door to the stair-well. She followed close behind as they climbed soundlessly to the second floor and let themselves into the interior hallway. Without slowing their stride, they kept right on walking.

Haskins paused briefly by the inner hallway door of apartment 25 and reaching above him, stuck the dime-sized listening bug on the wall above the door frame out of view.

Hardly missing a stride, he continued behind Cara and disappeared with her down the central hall separating the two lines of apartments. Then they trotted back down the stairs and let themselves outside into the snow.

Entry and exit had been accomplished successfully in less than three minutes. As the guys liked to say: it wasn't their first rodeo.

But they weren't finished yet.

Four vehicles sat in the parking lot, over a foot of snow mounded on top of them. One of them belonged to Peet and there was only one way to find out which one it was then search it.

A single security light flooded the lot on this side of the building. Normally, Cara would have made quick work of shooting out the light – even though apparently that was Haskins' specialty – but the neighborhood was, for all practical purposes, shut down. The storm worked to their advantage in that respect because neither of them was armed and disabling the light wasn't a possibility.

"Nothing like a little B&E to keep the skills up to snuff," Haskins muttered and after fishing around in one of the pouches on his pant leg, he produced his pick kit again.

"Make it fast," Cara said, providing over-watch for him.

"Small town America," Haskins said with a grunt. "This one's not even locked."

Cara ducked into the passenger seat of the small compact and dug around in the glove box while Haskins moved on to the next vehicle.

Per the registration, the car belonged to Kathy Becker.

She quickly ducked back out and closed the door behind her, ready to move on to the next on.

"This is Peet's," Haskins said as he stuck his head, up to his shoulders, into an older model gray, Ford Escort.

He reached under the steering wheel and popped the trunk.

While Haskins sifted through the contents of the interior of Peet's car, Cara quickly sorted through the assortment of garbage bags, boxes of tools and various junk littering his trunk.

"Anything?" Haskins asked, joining her.

"The guy's a slob," she muttered, "but there's nothing in here to indicate he's building a bomb or about to stage a nuclear energy plant takeover – mock or real. You find anything?"

"His vehicle registration is past due. Appears to be the biggest trouble he's got brewing."

"Better safe than sorry," Cara said, sorting through the last garbage bag, "but more and more I'm thinking these guys aren't much more than gamers."

"You sound disappointed."

She resealed the bag, shut the trunk and turned to him. "Anytime I can disprove an eminent threat, I'm a happy agent."

They usually weren't that lucky. The large percentage of the missions RRA deployed them on were the real deal. This one, however, looked more and more like a lost lead. And she'd be lying if she said she wasn't disappointed she was missing Christmas with her family because of it.

"Duck." Haskins grabbed her arm and pulled her down beside him behind the vehicle just as a pair of headlights cut a laser-like beam through the falling snow. A heavy-duty club-cab pickup truck came out of nowhere and pulled into the lot. Snow tires with studs explained how the vehicle was able to maneuver in this mess.

Cara scampered behind Haskins to the driver's side of the car to avoid being spotted. Hunkered low, they glanced at the tracks they'd made in over a foot of snow surrounding the car and mentally calculated their odds of being discovered.

The snow fell hard and thick and fast now. Depending on the focus of whoever had just parked, hopefully they'd be thinking about getting out of the cold, not their surroundings.

"This is so bogus," a man muttered after climbing out of the truck and slamming the door behind him.

"Chill." Another man said, followed by the slam of second truck door then two more in rapid succession. "Let's hear what he has to say, then let him know we make our own decisions. Hurry up. We need time to talk with Peet and Carson before Matthews gets here. Get our crap together to let Matthews know how it's going to be."

"His way, that's how it's going to be," a disgusted voice trailed off as the four men walked away from them.

Practically invisible in the deluge of snow, Cara and Haskins stayed in place for several seconds after they heard the four sets of footsteps climb the stairs to the second floor.

When the apartment door closed behind them, Haskins touched her arm. They had fresh Intel to gather and process and unless one of the men forgot something, there should be ample time to check it out.

With Cara watching his back, Haskins circled around to the passenger side of the pickup. The hood was still warm and the motor still ticking as he made quick work of the electric locks. Once inside, he rifled through the glove box then the console compartment between the bucket seats.

The box of the truck was topped with a fitted vinyl cover. Feeling secure that they were still in the clear, Cara slipped to the tailgate, lowered it, and checked inside just as Haskins climbed out of the cab, quietly shut the door behind him.

"It's finally gotten interesting," Cara said, as he joined her. A large molded gun case lay in the truck bed.

"Nice," Haskins remarked when they opened the case and found a bolt action hunting rifle equipped with a high powered scope. "Probably standard equipment in Iowa in the winter. Lots of deer hunters, I suspect."

He was right. While it would make a nice weapon, any terrorist worth their salt would be carrying an AK-47 or an AR-15 semi-automatic assault rifle.

Leaving the weapon, Cara closed then fastened the gun case and with Haskins' help, quietly closed the tail gate.

"Let's beat feet while our luck's still holding," Haskins said.

Ducking low, they circled the far side of the building so they couldn't be spotted from Peet's second floor windows and rushed back to the motel on a route that kept them out of view of the apartment and the single surveillance camera. Only when they were back inside the room, did they feel confident they hadn't been spotted.

* * *

Josh had snapped a photo of the truck's registration. Cara was on her phone now, relating the information to their contact, requesting details on one, Gary F. Scott, the only one of the four additional 'cell' members that they had Intel on.

Josh shrugged out of his Parka and pants and moved over to the table with all of their surveillance gear.

"Also, the name Matthews was mentioned by one of the men," Josh heard her say in the background. "See what you can find on any Matthews as it relates to environmental activism. From what I've gathered, he might be calling the shots and they aren't happy about it."

As she talked, Josh pulled a chair up to the table, linked

his cell phone to the coordinates on the listening device and plugged in a headset. "Let's see what we've got."

He was peripherally aware as Cara stripped down to her jeans and sweater then walked over beside him. "How's the reception?"

He held up a hand, his brow furrowed as he concentrated on adjusting the connection.

For several frustrating minutes, he struggled to pick anything up. He finally let out a defeated breath, removed the headset and unplugged them from his phone so the bugged conversation could be heard in the room.

Only there was nothing to hear. Nothing but static.

"What?" Cara frowned at him.

"Storm must be messing up the cell signal. I'm not picking up anything."

"Can we switch over to WiFi?"

"Worth a try." He disconnected from his phone and started hooking up to the laptop.

"Same thing. Gotta be the weather." He gave up after several minutes of trying. "Technology's great – when it works."

"We need to get back over there," Cara said. "Something's happening. We've gone from two to six. Seven when this Matthews person shows up. It's pretty clear that something big is going to happen between them."

"Probably a hot game of Dungeons and Dragons," Josh said cynically but he knew she was right. If they wanted to get in on what they were up to – a pajama party or a staged attack on an atomic power plant – they were going to have to do it the old-fashioned way.

"What are you doing?" she asked when he switched programs.

"RRA surely sent the specs for the apartment building."

When she nodded, he looked for the right file then pulled up the heating system and duct work information.

"Oh, crap," Cara muttered as she looked over his shoulder. "I hate heat ducts."

"Only because you know that you'll fit better than I will," Josh said, committing to memory the duct work path to apartment 25.

"Did I just get volunteered for this gig?"

She was already zipping into her white winter gear again when he closed the laptop and reached for his jacket. "You're the boss. It's your call."

CHAPTER SIX

Cara's heartbeat ticked up as Haskins boosted her up to the lip of the open heat duct situated near the ceiling of the first floor maintenance room. With a final push, she managed to pull herself inside.

It had taken him all of thirty seconds to break into the building again, access the maintenance room, then remove the protective grate that opened up to the network of HVAC runs feeding heat and AC to the entire building.

"Mic check," he said and when his voice came through her headset and he got a copy on hers, she was satisfied they had a good connection.

"There are disadvantages to being small," she muttered as she shimmied all the way into the duct, glad that she'd shucked her winter gear. "It's like a furnace in here," she sputtered.

He pushed out an amused chuckle. "Imagine that."

"Stop enjoying this so much. That's an order," she shot back at him and flipped on her head mounted flashlight.

"Have a good trip."

She expressed what she thought of that by muttering a few choice expletives under her breath.

"I didn't quite catch that."

She swore she heard another snicker of amusement. "I said, I love my job," she grumbled. "And you're disobeying a direct order."

Then she started crawling, all the time fighting back a niggling anxiety, as she stared ahead at what looked like miles of cramped metal tunnel. There was no time for a case of claustrophobia now.

"You solid on the route?" Haskins asked from below.

"Yeah, I got it."

For the next several long, uncomfortable minutes, she elbow-crawled, climbed, twisted and turned, relying on her memory and Haskins' voice in her ear to guide her. By the time she could see light at the end of the tunnel – the wall grate that fed heat and AC to Apartment 25 - she was hot, out of breath and fighting claustrophobia again.

Finally, she made it to the duct that lead directly to the apartment. She carefully turned the corner then for a short moment, let herself catch her breath, cool down and regroup. Steady again, she shut off her flashlight and crawled the last ten feet to the end of the duct.

"In position," she whispered into her mic. "Stand by."

"Roger that."

He was all business now and Haskins' rock solid tone helped steady her. His voice had always had that effect on her. If they were in a speed boat bouncing across monster swells in the ocean, or in the desert, their camouflage gear and a few sand dunes the only things hiding them from the enemy, or in the jungle heat, a palm frond their only cover, his voice, steady, confident, and true north, helped her keep her bearings and her nerve.

Not that this little adventure in HVAC hell compared to

live ammo and full on combat, but, still, a reassuring presence on the other end of her lifeline helped keep her focused and calm.

She gathered herself on a deep breath, then lifted her head and squinted through the thin slats in the metal grate and down into the room.

Eight feet below, six men sat or stood or paced around a kitchen table. She could barely detect a dime's worth of difference in physical characteristics between them from this angle. All early to late twenties, dark, overly-long hair, 5' 6" to 5' 8" feet tall, maybe. While she tried to avoid profiling, it was impossible not to with these guys. They had insecure, nerd gamers written all over them. The way they walked, carried themselves – even down to their skin tight jeans and button down shirts.

She reached carefully into her breast pocket and pulled out a small camera, no bigger than a flash drive. Methodically circling the table, she snapped several photos of each individual, only satisfied when she'd gotten either full face shots or profiles of those who had their backs to her. She'd transmit them back to RRA HQ later.

"They're pretty quiet," she whispered into her mic.

Brad Carson stood abruptly, his chair scraping loudly on the floor. "What was that?"

Cara shrank back from the grate, afraid he'd heard her.

For several long seconds, the only thing breaking the silence was her pounding heart.

———

"You're spooky as a damn deer, Carson," Peet complained. "Just chill, man. We've got this. When Matthews comes, we tell him we're out. Solid front. All six of us. He can't argue with that."

"The hell he can't." Brad glared from Chad to Max, the Miller brothers, one as gullible and malleable as the other. Max was nervous, too. Scared.

"Matthews is crazy," Chad said. "And he thinks we're on board."

"And whose fault is that?" Brad all but shouted, his gaze landing on Peet.

"You can't pin this on me," Peet protested, sounding defensive and jittery.

Brad didn't figure that now was the time to mince words. He'd once looked upon Peet as his mentor, but since he'd brought Matthews into the group, he only saw Peet as a screw up. "You're the one who asked him to join our group. Am I right?"

"How the hell was I supposed to know he was nuts?" Peet pushed up and away from the table. He dragged a hand through his unkempt hair. "And I didn't see any of you asking him to leave. Well, did I?" His angry gaze scanned the other group members.

"Besides," Peet continued, "none of that matters now. What matters is that we let him know how we feel."

"So we tell a crazy man that we think he's crazy?" Gary shook his head. "That's going to go over real well."

"Look," Roger attempted calm. "There are six of us. It's *our* group. Matthews is the outsider. We tell him that we were wrong. That we got caught up in his idea but the longer we've thought about it, the more we realize that we don't want to get involved. Easy Peasy. It's not like he's a commando or something. Cripes. He's over twice our age. What can he do to us?"

"He could shoot us," Brad pointed out.

"Oh, for God's sake. He's not going to shoot us," Peet said. "He's not a killer. He's an activist. He's not going to hurt anyone. You're letting yourself get worked up over nothing."

"Nothing?" Brad said, incredulous. "He wants to attack a nuclear power plant."

"Stage an attack. Big difference. For all we know he's all talk no action," Peet argued glancing around the room. "The guy's delusional. He's just playing at being tough. We tell him no, he'll pick up his toys and go home."

"Where is home anyway?" Roger wondered aloud. "I mean, where did he come from? He just showed up out of the blue. Has he ever said where he lives?"

They all looked at each other, shrugged.

"Seems strange."

"Everything about Matthews is strange," Brad muttered. "He scares the bejesus out of me."

"Let's back up the truck," Max interjected thoughtfully. "We gave him more than enough hints last time we met that we're conflicted about his idea."

"Conflicted?" Brad laughed bitterly. "Oh, that's rich. Not one of us had the balls to tell him we were out."

"We'll tell him tonight." Peet looked resolute. "As a group. Okay?

"Okay?" he repeated pointedly when they looked at each other.

A loud knock made them all jump like scared rabbits, then jerk all eyes toward the door.

MOCK ATTACK. Stupid. Not entirely surprised, not wholly relieved, Cara backed a few feet away from the grate. "Almost wish they were jihadists," she whispered into her mic. "These yahoos are planning to stage a mock attack at the nuclear plant."

"Well, I guess I've had worse news," Haskins muttered in her ear.

"Let me rephrase that. They did want to stage a fake attack, but now they don't. They want to deep six the idea but this Matthews person, who hasn't arrived yet, is the one pushing it. They've all had an epiphany and plan to tell him they want out – but they're afraid of him."

"Big brave terrorists."

Cara could picture Haskins shaking his head in disgust.

"Yeah. And not a problem. Something about this Matthews character though, has them quaking in their Birkenstocks. I think he's got a lot of power over them.

"Wait," she whispered abruptly. "Someone just knocked on the door. Could be Matthews. Gotta go."

"Hold on a sec. If it's this Matthews character, he probably drove here. Will you be okay for a few minutes while I go out and search his vehicle?"

"Yes. Go. Just hurry back."

AFTER A LONG GLANCE around the room, Peet wiped damp palms on his thighs then walked to the door.

When he swung it open, Matthews barged in, shoving Jeannie Pruitt roughly ahead of him.

Brad felt his heart go haywire. For a moment, no one said a word. They all stared in disbelief, too shocked to move.

"What ... what are you doing?" Brad couldn't keep his eyes off Jeannie.

She was gagged and her hands were bound behind her back. The middle-aged woman's eyes shined wild with fear. Matthews had tightly tied a scarf around her mouth; snow dusted her dyed black hair that stuck out in little tufts around her face where it wasn't crushed beneath the scarf.

Tears leaked down Jeannie's cheeks. Her eyes pleaded with Brad to help her.

"Stop. Matthews. You're hurting her!" Brad finally found his voice again.

Matthews ignored him and shoved her to her knees. She cried out in pain. With his hand pushing her head toward the floor, he reached into his pocket for a pack of cigarettes, shook one out and lit up.

"For God's sake. Let her go." Brad knotted his hair in both hands, still not believing what was happening. "This is crazy! You're crazy."

"I'm not crazy, boys. I'm betrayed. We're all betrayed. Jeannie's had a change of heart."

Matthews looked around the small room. "She wants to back out."

Even though his gaze was steady, his stance was anxious and edgy, like he was about one deep breath away from exploding.

"Can you believe it? She says she wants out. Doesn't want to help us anymore. What do you think about that?"

Jeannie whimpered and Brad drilled his gaze on Matthews. His gut rolled. He clenched his fists on his thighs.

"So what?" Brad challenged. "So she doesn't want to help. That's her option. You ... you can't treat her like this."

He moved to help Jeannie up.

Matthews shoved him away. "Leave her be."

Brad stumbled backwards. Max caught him before he fell.

"There have got to be consequences for turning on the group. Agreed?" Matthews gaze pierced like a knife as he searched each man's face.

No one said a word. One by one, they cast their eyes downward. Only Brad glared back at him, but finally looked away as the black rage in Matthews's gaze intensified.

"None of you boys are thinking about backing out, are you?"

Silence, as loud as a freight train, filled the room.

A long, warning silence.

It was clear that Matthews sensed an undercurrent of rebellion.

"What do you think we should do about Jeannie's betrayal?"

Again, he waited. And Brad felt a fear and sense of doom unlike any he'd ever known. For the first time in years, he prayed. For Jeannie and for them ... for whoever got in Matthews' way.

He breathed deep, focused on Jeannie. Terrified for her. She was the true pawn in all of this. She was a security guard at the nuclear plant. Matthews had targeted her, made her think he was interested in her. For a widow with limited income, working for the time when she could retire on a pension, the attention Matthews had given her was more than any man had given her since her husband died ten years ago.

He'd turned her head. Taken her on dates. Brought her flowers. Then he'd brought her to a meeting.

"This is Jeannie," Matthews had said, beaming down at her, squeezing her against him as he'd proudly announced to the group, "She's our golden ticket."

He'd pressed a tender kiss to her temple and Jeannie had reddened like a school girl with her first crush, completely under Matthews' spell. "Pretty Jeannie knows everything there is to know about the plant security."

Pretty Jeannie didn't look so pretty right now. She looked terrified as she knelt on the tile floor. Muffled sobs punctuated that terror.

"I asked you what we should do about her?" he repeated. "No ideas? Not one of you?"

Matthews's livid tone brought Brad's head up to see the older man toss his half burned cigarette on the floor, grind it out with his boot heel, then draw a handgun out from his belt at the small of his back.

Brad's heart stopped. He glanced around the room, certain someone would say something. No one did. They were all practically pissing their pants with fear.

"Wait!" Brad yelled. "What … what are you going to do?" he stammered as Matthews fished a sound suppressor out of his pocket and affixed it to the barrel of the gun.

"Noooooo!!" Brad screamed as Matthews pointed the gun at the back of Jeannie's head and pulled the trigger.

CHAPTER SEVEN

Cara sucked in a breath, then held it after the gun went off. Disbelieving she'd just witnessed an assassination.

A chorus of gasps followed the gunshot, then the thump of a body hitting the floor.

Matthews had shot the woman. The crazy SOB had executed her.

She looked down at the men, who stood motionless with shock, as blood pooled around the woman's head.

"Don't worry. We really didn't need her anymore anyway. I got all the information from her I needed," Matthews interjected to the room at large. "And had a good time in the process, if you know what I mean."

Oh, he was a terrorist all right. Cara could deliver a profile and not miss a detail. He was a cold blooded killer. Methodical and manipulative. And hovering around the fringe of insanity. And right now, unarmed, she was as sure as dead if she opened her mouth. She couldn't do a single thing to stop him from whatever madness he had in mind. And what he had in mind, she was now certain, was not a fake attack. He was in this for real.

"Well..."

Matthews's voice drew her back to the kitchen and the gruesome death scene below.

"Are we ready to do this?"

"To ... tonight?" Peel squeaked. "You want to stage the attack ...tonight?"

"No better night than tonight. In this weather, there won't be a city cop or a county deputy within an hour of the plant. We've got 4-wheel drive trucks, one equipped with a snow blade, duel tires and chains. We can go anywhere we want unimpeded. So yes, we move tonight."

So much for recon, Cara muttered under her breath and tried to reach Haskins via her mic. She couldn't raise him on the radio. He must still be outside.

They were way past recon now. They were full on intercept and overcome a terrorist plot that could potentially kill millions of people and contaminate the most essential water source in the heartland of the United States.

Matthews' ruthless and brutal murder of a woman he had used and mined for information, proved he was capable of anything. So yeah, it had become painfully clear; Matthews wasn't going to the extreme length of killing a woman to stage a mock attack.

This guy was playing for real.

The question now was, what was his reluctant team of terrorists going to do? Would they follow through with their pact to tell Matthews they were out, or would the woman's assassination get the results Matthews had clearly wanted? Would fear for their own lives make them unwilling accomplices?

Where was Haskins? She needed to talk with him. She tried to reach him again. Swore under her breath when, again, she got no response.

WHEN JOSH SLIPPED OUT of the apartment building, he swore that during the hour or less Cara had been eavesdropping on the conversation in Peet's apartment, another foot or more of snow had fallen. The temperature had dropped as well and the wind had picked up, making a screeching, banshee wail as it whipped between the buildings, swirling up mini-tornadoes of snow in its wake.

His southern blood felt frozen. How do these people live in this weather, he wondered as he rounded the building, braced himself against the wind and peeked through the blinding snow toward the parking lot.

As best as he could make out, it was still empty of people and the only new vehicle in the lot was another heavy-duty pickup equipped with a snow blade, duel rear tires and chains. There were probably shovels and sand bags under the tarp that covered the truck bed as well.

Couldn't say these boys weren't prepared for winter.

Ducking low to be on the safe side, and bucking the wind, he slogged through twenty plus inches of snow now covering the lot. After brushing the snow off the door handle of the newly arrived truck, he got out his kit. It took a little longer to break in this time. The truck was a newer model and loaded with extras. Plus the weather was definitely working against him.

His fingers felt stiff and frozen when he finally fudged the lock and cracked open the door. Hauling himself up on the running board, he ducked inside, closing the door behind him.

Holding his penlight between his teeth, he rifled through the glove box until he found the vehicle registration. Then he hit the jackpot. Five driver's licenses under five different names. Only one was under the name of Matthews. Trent Matthews, supposedly of Chicago, Illinois.

Only someone up to no good needed multiple ID's and driver's licenses. Which meant that things might just be starting to get real. He fished into his breast pocket for his phone, snapped a picture of the license and made a decision to send the pic to RRA directly without clearing it through Cara first. They needed to ID this Matthews guy – or whatever his name was - and see if he was on anyone's radar.

Josh was starting to get a really bad feeling about this. Why was a fifty something man, allegedly from Chicago, hanging around with a bunch of twenty something gullible gamers from small town Iowa?

Could be Josh had just answered his own question. They were gullible. And 'Matthews' was old enough to use that gullibility to his advantage.

Josh wanted info on this guy and he wanted it fast. He also wanted to get a look at what was under the tarp covering the truck bed. He'd just hit the send button on his phone when the passenger door flew open and a closed fist shot straight toward his face.

Surprise slowed his reflexes. The punch landed hard and high on his cheek, rattling his teeth before someone else grabbed him by the front of his parka, dragged him out of the truck and threw him to his back on the ground.

He landed with an explosion of pain. If the deep snow hadn't partially broken his fall he'd be spitting teeth and nursing a concussion.

Self-preservation instincts kicked in as his head started to clear. He grasped his attacker's arms and rolled until he was straddling him. He drew his hand back to throw a punch ... and white hot pain burst through the back of his head.

He collapsed, face first, in the snow. Fighting the pain and to keep from passing out, he strained to push himself to his knees - then froze, recognizing the unmistakable feel of the business end of a gun barrel pressed against his cheek.

Someone on his other side racked the slide on an automatic pistol – making it clear that he was both outnumbered and out gunned and that whoever they were, they meant business.

"Now would be a good time to say uncle."

Not in this lifetime.

Still, he was with the program enough to realize that his chances of out muscling them were exactly slim and none. Fighting dizziness, he struggled to his knees. Blood dripped crimson red from the cut in his cheek into the snow.

He slowly raised his hands in surrender.

For now.

Now that he was upright he could see what he was up against and took a quick head count. There were four of them. All armed. His lucky day.

"Get on your feet," the guy with what he recognized as a Glock 23 ordered.

He tried. But his knees were rubber. His head screamed foul. He collapsed, again, in the snow.

"Get him up," one of them ordered.

Two men grabbed him and hauled him to his feet. Then they walked him to the apartment and half-shoved, half-carried him up the outside stairs. They didn't stop until they were in front of Peet's apartment door.

Josh was in bad shape, but not as bad as he let on. As long as they thought he was only half with the program, he had a shred of an advantage.

But when someone opened the door to their knock, his reaction to the grisly sight inside, gave him away.

"WHAT THE HELL IS THIS?" Matthews's face turned blotchy red with rage when the apartment door flew open and several men barged in. "What are you doing up here? You were supposed to wait outside."

Brad's sense of doom quadrupled. He saw guns. Lots of them. And five more men. All of them, apparently, were with Matthews. All but the one being held at gunpoint.

He almost passed out with fear. He couldn't stop thinking about Jeannie. Couldn't stop looking at her dead body, at the blood pooled around her head.

This was so bad. So freaking bad. He didn't know any of the men. Couldn't see the face of the man dressed all in white. Until one of them ripped off his face mask and hood.

The blood drained from his face. He leaned back against the wall to keep on his feet. It was the guy from the restaurant. The one with the hot babe.

What was he doing here? And why were they pointing a gun at him? Blood oozed out of a cut high on his cheek and ran down his face. Someone had hit him. Hard enough that he was weaving on his feet.

"Explain," Matthews barked.

"Found him snooping around in your truck." The guy with the Glock answered.

At least Brad thought he recognized it as a Glock.

"In my truck?" Matthews stalked up to their hostage. "You want to tell me what you were doing?"

"Just ... just getting warm, man. Until these--"

Matthews punched him hard in the diaphragm.

The guy crumpled with an oomph of pain. The only thing keeping him upright were the two guys holding him.

"Try again," Matthews ordered.

"My ... mistake. Thought ... it was my truck--"

Another gut punch.

This one buckled his knees on a groan of intense pain.

Brad figured he would have crumpled to the floor if the two guys hadn't hauled him back up again.

"Think carefully before you open your mouth again." Matthews grabbed his hair and jerked his head up. Got right in his face. "Third strike and you're out. So do better this time."

"Okay. O ... kay," the guy grunted out, clearly struggling for breath. "I was ... delivering a ... a present from Santa. Now you've ... ruined the surprise."

Brad could see Matthews's rage building to a boiling point. Whoever this guy was, he was a tough SOB. Tough and possibly stupid. Matthews hadn't hesitated to kill Jeannie. This guy was as good as dead.

"Anybody here know him?" Matthews said in a deadly quiet voice, never taking his eyes off of hostage as he pulled his pistol from behind his back again.

"Anybody?" Matthews shouted, spinning around to face them, when he didn't get an answer.

Everyone shook their head. Everyone but Brad. Something kept him from responding.

"You. Carson." Matthews walked over to him. "You know something."

Brad shook his head. "No ... no I don't know him. But I recognize him." Brad swallowed. "He ... he was in the restaurant earlier. Ate a pizza."

Brad swallowed hard as Matthews looked from him back to the hostage. "Damned if that's not a coincidence. Anyone with him?"

Brad cut a quick glance at the guy. Saw the plea in his eyes. The slight shake of his head. And he thought of the pretty blond and the fate she might come to if he told Matthews about her.

"No. He ... he was alone. Said his flight out of Cedar Rapids was canceled. That's all. He ate then he left."

"You see where he went?"

Brad shook his head, another risk but he wasn't going to tell Matthews that they were staying at the motel because he'd head straight there and most likely find the blond and she was too pretty for Matthews to kill.

"This might tell you something, boss." Glock guy, big and burly and as mean looking as a badger, handed Matthews a phone. "He dropped it when I dragged him out of the truck."

Matthews took the phone, glared at it and handed it back. "It's smashed."

"Yeah. That's kind of how I found it ... I stepped on it. It was hidden in the snow."

Matthews glanced at the fourth guy. He was tall and skinny with an Ichabod Crane face, and he gripped an assault rifle as if he'd been born with it in his hand. "Can you pull any information off of this?"

Ichabod reached for the broken phone, turned it over in his hand. "Maybe. Take a while though."

"We don't have a while if we want to take advantage of this weather." Matthews turned back to the guy who was still hanging his head and trying to catch his breath.

"Back to that third strike. You just became interesting. Which means you dodged a bullet. You're alive until I find out who you are and why you were in my truck.

"Dump him on the floor. Tie him up. We'll deal with him when we get back." Matthews turned back to Peet. "You ready to go?"

Peet closed his eyes. Swallowed. "Um ..."

Oh, God, Brad thought. *You can't say no now, Peet. Not after he killed Jeannie. If you do, we're all as dead as she is.*

Through his panic, Brad had been forming a plan in his mind. They'd agree to go. They'd all pile into Max's truck, follow Matthews for a few blocks, then peel off and drive like hell to the Police station and warn them. They'd save themselves and the nuc plant, too.

If everything went right. A big if.

"Um?" Matthews said mockingly. "Um, what?"

Peet's gaze darted around the room, seeking support and courage from the others. He got neither.

"You weren't thinking of backing out on me? Like dead Jeannie backed out?"

Peet glanced guiltily at Matthews then hung his head. "Do you need us now? This wasn't supposed to be for real, man. No one was supposed to ... to get hurt. Or ... or killed..."

"We're with you!" Brad spoke up quickly to shut Peet up.

All of them - Peet, Max, Chad, Gary, and Roger – cut their gazes toward him, their eyes big and round and surprised.

Matthews looked from Brad to Peet then to the others, trying to read their thoughts with narrowed eyes.

"Looks like you just surprised your buddies. You sure that's your plan? Or are you planning to back out?"

"No," Brad said quickly. "We're with you."

Brad could see in Matthews' eyes that he hadn't bought the lie.

"You know what?" Matthews smiled. "It's okay. Peet's right. I really don't need you guys anymore either. You don't have to go."

No one breathed a sigh of relief. They may have been gullible but they weren't stupid.

"I just needed your brilliant plan. And you brought it to life for me. What I can't figure, is how you can be so brainy and yet so easy to dupe."

When he drew the gun up and pointed the silenced barrel at Peet, Brad knew they were all dead men.

CHAPTER EIGHT

CARA HAD BEEN HOLDING her breath for what seemed like a decade. From the moment Matthews's men dragged Haskins inside, semi-conscious and bleeding, she'd watched, powerless to do anything to help him. She was unarmed. Outnumbered.

Helpless.

The word echoed around in her mind, momentarily draining her of calm and reason. She'd confronted countless enemies over her military career. But she'd never been in a position where the scales were this unbalanced. She had a pocket knife. That was it. Nothing to fight them with. No way to save Haskins or even herself for that matter.

Right now it was Haskins she was worried about. She had to do something. Anything to diffuse the situation. Create a diversion to give him a chance to escape or to disarm them. Give him a fighting chance.

Which meant she had to leave the heat vent. She had to leave Haskins knowing that any number of things could happen to him while she was scurrying back to the maintenance room to pull the fire alarm or cut the lights. Anything to create confusion and give Haskins a chance to escape or overtake them until she could get there to help.

She could not lose him. Not now. Not now that she knew the unthinkable. She loved the man.

The thought registered like a bomb then scattered like vapor into the tight vent. *She loved him.*

All right. Fine. The admission terrified her. But right now she was more terrified by the thought of losing him.

Containing her panic, and burying her unexpected truth in the back of her mind, she backed away from the grate as quietly and as fast as she could.

And then she heard the first shot.

A man screamed. Another whimpered. Another begged.

She froze, whispered a tortured "no" then flinched with each of the five successive shots.

She closed her eyes. Then collapsed, boneless, when one more shot blasted into the echoing stillness and crushed any hope that Haskins had escaped the mass execution.

Clenching her teeth to keep from crying out, she dug deep for a small kernel of hope. She knew Haskins. She knew he was a survivor. He could still be alive. All of them could be alive, she told herself, refusing to consider that she was too late to save him or any of others if she could get to them and keep them from bleeding out.

Dreading what she would find, she crept on elbows and knees back to the grate. Listened.

Prayed for the impossible.

Just as she reached the grate, she heard Matthews's voice.

"All right, funny man. Do you understand now what happens to people who aren't straight up with me?"

Making its way through the rubble of despair, hope shot Cara's pulse up by several beats. He had to be talking to Haskins.

"Do you understand?" Matthews repeated and just as she peeked down into the room, he kicked Haskins in the ribs.

He was alive! That fact, above all others, registered even as Haskins grunted in pain and slumped sideways to the floor.

"Now let's try again," Matthews feigned patience. "What were you doing in my truck?"

Haskins didn't respond.

"He's passed out, boss," one of them said after getting no reaction when he poked Haskins with the toe of his boot. "You want me to wake him up?"

Matthews stared at Haskins for a long moment then shook his head. "No. We'll leave him on ice for a while. Make sure both his hands and feet are cuffed up tight. And gag him. If he's still alive after we finish the job, we'll find out who he works for.

"Something about him bugs me," he added while Cara's heart slammed with the need to get into that room and help him.

She held her breath while Matthews scowled down on Haskins' limp body. "I don't know what it is but he's not just some guy off the street. Something about him says military. Maybe special operations," he added with a narrowed scowl. "Somebody might want him back. Who knows, he could make for a great negotiating tool. And trust me, after we're finished with that nuc plant, there's going to be a boatload of alphabet agencies wanting to make a deal to keep us from breaching another one."

<hr />

HEART POUNDING, Cara waited for the five men to walk out of the apartment, close, and lock the door behind them.

On a serrated breath, she squeezed her eyes shut and prayed. Please, please let him just be unconscious, not dead.

But he was so still. Too still.

When she got a full view of the room, she gasped, felt herself pale at the carnage. Those young vulnerable men ... all six of them lay on the floor, their blood splattered on the walls, pooling beneath their lifeless bodies. No signs of life among them or the woman who had been an innocent, defenseless and duped.

Cara was no stranger to death. Knew what it felt like to witness the atrocities of man. She had nightmares over every life she'd taken, saw them as mother's sons even though the men she'd had to kill to protect and defend had been monsters.

It never got easy. Facing death. Causing death. Witnessing death. For several moments the scene below in that room paralyzed her.

The thought of the one man who might still be living, needing her help, moved her into action. She needed to get to Haskins.

She pushed at the grate with all of her might. It wouldn't budge. She pounded on it. Rammed it with the flat of her hands. Bloodied her closed fists on it, and still, it wouldn't give.

There was only one hope of forcing it loose and getting into the room and to Haskins without making the long trip back to the maintenance room through the vent system. She had to kick it out. To do that, she had to get turned around.

"Haskins," she whispered, not wanting to startle him if he was conscious. "Haskins," she said louder when he didn't respond. Concern kicked her in the gut. "Haskins if you can hear me, I'll be right back."

She backed out of the vent as fast as she could, bruising her elbows and knees and banging her head. When she'd advanced ten feet backwards, she met the T-bone in the duct system. Squirming to her side, she made her body into a C shape, shimmied and scooted and finally got herself turned around. Then she crawled backwards on her stomach until she reached the grate again.

Then she kicked. And kicked some more, loading all of her pent up rage and fear into it. Still no give. She needed better leverage and to do that, she had to be on her back. On a groan of frustration, she struggled and wriggled and squirmed from her stomach to her back. Winded but running on a surge of adrenaline, and definitely getting a better angle, she kicked with all her strength.

On her very first kick, the grate budged. Her heart leaped with excitement.

Five more hard kicks and it gave way, let go and fell free, rattling on the floor where it landed. The hole was just wide enough for her to slip through it.

She wouldn't be any help to Haskins if she broke her back from the fall though. She needed to get back to her stomach again. Hot and sweating, pushing her physical limits, but still fueled by adrenaline, she finally got herself turned over.

On a deep breath she backed up until her legs, then her hips slid through the hole and into the kitchen. On a bracing breath, she pushed herself the rest of the way out and dropped the seven feet to the floor.

She landed off balance, fell sideways ... and just shy of Brad Carson's body. Forcing herself to ignore the slaughter, she half-crawled half-fell onto Haskins thighs.

The impact jolted him toward consciousness. He groaned. His head rolled on his shoulders.

His slight movement was all she needed to bolster her strength. "Thank God!"

She rose to her knees beside him, untied his gag and then cut the flex cuffs around his wrists and feet with her pocket knife. "Come on open those eyes for me. I need to see them."

Needing all of her strength, she pulled and tugged and

finally got him shifted so he was sitting up with his back against the wall. He groaned again, then blinked slowly down at her, his gaze muzzy and confused before his eyes slid closed again.

Cara was so overcome with relief that he was alive and responsive, she swung her leg over his thighs and straddled his lap.

"Haskins," she whispered, then cupped his face between her hands and kissed him, pouring all of her relief and love into the kiss as if she could fill him with it.

She finally pulled back and pressed her forehead to his, overwhelmed with relief. "I knew you were too tough to die on me."

Tears trickled down her cheeks when he groaned again. She pulled back and wiped her thumb across the blood dried on his bruised and bleeding face. "Wake up, tough guy. Come on. I need you. You have to pull it together."

He blinked at her again, clearly fighting to get her into focus – then one corner of his mouth quirked up when he realized it was her.

"What ... took you ... so long? Sir."

"ARE YOU SURE YOU'RE OKAY?" On her knees, working her way among the bodies, Cara checked for any sign of life.

He was not okay, Josh admitted to himself. But he was getting there. "I'm fine. Let's go."

As soon as he'd come around enough that he could move his head without keeling over, Cara had helped him struggle to his feet. Now, still a little woozy, he leaned against the wall, watching her.

She finally stood, her grisly task over. Tears filled her eyes when she met his. Shook her head. "Nothing. They're all dead."

Josh clenched his jaw, brimming with rage. Matthews – or whatever his name was – was a savage. He'd killed those boys – he couldn't think of them as men – without one second of hesitation.

"Let's go." He pushed himself away from the wall. Almost went down before she lunged for him and held him steady. Slinging his arm over her shoulder for support, they started toward the door.

"Wait." She stopped abruptly and dug into her pocket when her phone vibrated.

"Graves," she answered. "Yeah. No. He's with me. He's hurt, but he'll be okay."

RRA HQ no doubt. Calling Cara to find out what happened to him when they tried to respond to his text with Matthews' picture. Nothing rattles the brass like a missed check-in or an unanswered phone.

A brick, that's what had happened. Slammed into the back of his head. At least that's what it had felt like. Damn. His head pounded like a bitch. He leaned heavily against the wall and Cara, half-listening to her side of the conversation, as she told them what they'd discovered and the seven people Matthews had assassinated.

Then she listened, pinching her brows and closing her eyes in concentration. It could have been thirty seconds. Could have been an hour before she ended the call. He felt like he was hovering somewhere between now and nowhere, trying to get his brain synapses working.

Someone had gotten the drop on him.

Knocked him out.

Dragged him into the apartment.

Murdered a woman and those six boys.

Cara had kissed him.

Whoa.

That thought jolted him closer to full alert.

Cara had kissed him.

He looked at her hard when she disconnected.

"Between NSA, RRA and Department of Defense and Homeland Security, a hundred wheels have been set into motion. The Palo plant has been notified of an eminent threat and are in the process of locking down under a code red."

She stopped abruptly, touched a hand to his forehead. "What? Are you sure you're doing okay?"

"You kissed me?"

Her eyes went wide. Then she squared her shoulders and went all CO on him. "You contacted RRA without clearing it with me?"

Okay, then. They weren't going to talk about the kiss.

"Um ... you weren't exactly available," he pointed out, wondering how many demotions he'd get for abandoning protocol.

Really?

"Well ... " She pocketed her phone. "It was a good call. They ran the pic you took of Matthews' driver's licenses through our facial recognition program."

"*One* of his drivers licenses. *One* of his names." The fog was gradually clearing. "I found a fist full of licenses with various IDs. Who is he? Really?"

"Jacob Collins - aka Trent Matthews and a dozen other aliases — all of them connected to a series of international bombings with high death tolls. They go way back. Never solved.

"According to RRA," she continued, "no one knows his real ID. He's a ghost. Turns up near the attack sites before or soon after the destruction. Disappears right after. No one —

not Mossad, not MI-6, not the CIA, has been able to get a trail on this guy."

"And he ends up in Iowa of all places?"

"Fits his MO based on what they've told me. He selects his quarry based on their lack of notability instead of selecting more well known targets. You can anticipate attacks on target rich environments. Prepare for them. But if it's not even on anyone's radar, it's that much more vulnerable."

"Which would have been the case again this time, if Brad and the others hadn't stumbled back out onto the web, playing their activist games." He massaged his throbbing temples. "The good news in all this? If Matthews hadn't found them, used them, then we wouldn't have found Matthews."

"This is the first time anyone has even been close to stopping him. We just have to figure out how to do it."

"Yeah," Haskins said, holding his head. "Us and what army, again? Oh, yeah. Just us."

Matthews, or whatever his name was, was totally off the rails. He'd killed that woman. And those boys. Just ... executed them. Shot them point blank. Because they'd disappointed him. Because he could.

Maybe they won't have died in vain, Josh thought. Maybe because of them, he and Cara could take this monster out of commission for good.

"He's not going to get away with this," Cara promised him, as if she'd read his mind. "He's not going to kill another soul. Not on our watch."

She looked and sounded so fierce. Josh couldn't help but feel a rush of pride. Like he was always proud of her as she led their missions. She always handled one complication after another.

As for complications. He kept coming back to that moment. She'd kissed him. After they'd agreed that there could be nothing between them. Only the mission connected them. Only the mission mattered.

"Why are you looking at me like that?" she asked and only then did he realize he was staring.

"Are you okay? Do you think you have a concussion?"

"No. No concussion. Unless you tell me that I imagined it."

Her look shifted from concern to reluctant understanding. She knew exactly what he was referring to.

"No," she said tentatively. "You didn't imagine it."

He searched her eyes then drew her closer, tipping her face up to his. And kissed her. Pouring into that kiss, all the emotion he wouldn't let himself express in words. All the love he wasn't certain she was ready to know about. God knew, he wasn't sure if he was ready either.

When he drew away, her eyes were closed, her lips parted and bee stung and so tempting he went back for another kiss.

Soft. Tender. Filled with longing.

"I didn't imagine that, either, did I?" he whispered when he pulled away.

"No," she whispered back. "No, you didn't."

"To be continued." He pressed his lips to her forehead and pushed away from the wall. "Now let's go get those bastards."

CEDAR RAPIDS 9 NEWS

December 23rd, 5:20 pm

The KCRG TV 9 nightly news director counted off on his fingers ... 3, 2, 1 ...

....then pointed at Camera Four to zoom in on Don McDowell.

"Good evening, folks. I'm Don McDowell, your KCRG TV 9 first alert weatherman here to give you the latest update on our weather situation.

"I'm sure you remember that only yesterday we were on the fence about whether the blizzard, affectionately known as Holly, was going to be a no show or grace us with her presence here in East Central Iowa.

"Clearly, she's arriving with bells on! It's going to get nasty folks, and here's why."

Looking properly sober and concerned, Don rose from his desk and walked over in front of the animated weather screen. "If you look at this high pressure system here, you can see that it abruptly changed course and is pushing the storm our way at a very fast clip. So fast that the leading edge of this monster system has already arrived at our back door.

"If Holly stays on her current course, we're looking for her to dump another three to four feet of that white stuff in the next one to two hours. That's right. That's how fast she's moving.

"To add to the mix, pushing that snow are sustained winds clocked at thirty miles an hour with recorded gusts up to fifty. Holly is not a storm to take lightly. We're talking about dangerous wind chills of twenty to thirty degrees below zero. Visibility will be no farther than the hand in front of your face and heavy drifting is going to make travel not only unadvised but prohibited unless you're faced with an emergency."

Don turned back to the camera. "In fact, the Department of Transportation has asked TV 9 to relay that they've pulled snowplows off the road. So please heed these travel warnings and stay home unless you absolutely have to leave.

"Now we know there are bound to be emergencies and the CRPD and Linn County Sheriff's office have also asked us to request your complete cooperation in staying off the roads. Should you have such an emergency, call 911 as always, but be aware that the response time may be slower than usual.

"It's also possible that the strong winds may down trees and electrical wires so power outages are a real concern. For those of you who don't have an alternative heating source, be prepared to go to a neighbor's or a close by relative's because these temperatures are going to be dangerously low considering the wind chill. So folks, do check on your elderly neighbors and friends.

"Least you think it's all bad news here, we do have some good news for you." He turned back to the screen and with a click of his remote pulled up a twenty-four-hour map.

"Holly will blow out of Eastern Iowa almost as quickly as

she blew in. By tomorrow afternoon, just in time for Christmas Eve, we should have blue skies and normal winter temperatures in the mid to upper twenties.

"I'll leave you with this hope that Holly doesn't leave a path of destruction in her wake and you fine folks will be able to enjoy your holiday celebrations with your friends and families.

"Stay tuned to KCRG TV 9 for all of the latest weather updates and bulletins. Have a great rest of your evening and all day tomorrow."

CHAPTER NINE

JOSH STUMBLED out of the apartment, leaning heavily on Cara for support.

"Holy hell," he swore when the bitter cold and howling wind slammed against them, doing its best to knock them back against the door.

"Grab the railing," she shouted and with as much luck as perseverance, they made it to the bottom without falling. But just barely.

Snow drifts topping out at three feet met them. Walking wasn't possible. They waded. They slogged. They pushed on but even with Cara's help, the effort sapped his energy stockpile, that was already running on fumes.

He'd swam for his life in five foot ocean swells with rain beating down like buckshot; he'd led a charge through an Iraqi desert in a sand storm that had peeled the skin off his face. He was no stranger to severe weather or rough terrain. But this snow and wind and cold combined did its damnedest to take him down and keep him there.

"Just a few more ... steps," Cara shouted so he could hear her above the wind as she, too, struggled with her breath.

"We can do this! Just keep pushing."

So he did. For her. Because if not for her, he'd be flat on his face.

They finally reached the pickup that belonged to one of the dead men and fell against it. They'd trudged all of twenty feet. It felt like twenty miles.

He didn't know how she found the strength to help him up and into the passenger side of the truck, then wade through snow that was over her knees to get back to the driver's side and pulled herself up and in.

"My, God. It's freezing." She sucked in air, shivering as she dug into a pocket and pulled out a set of keys.

A surge of pride swamped him. Not only had she single-handedly hauled his sorry self down a flight of slippery stairs and muscled him to the truck, she was always thinking. As difficult as it had been for her to check each body for signs of life, she'd been thinking ahead and found keys for the truck, knowing it was their only hope of following Matthews.

Despite the raw temperature, the engine turned over on the first try.

Relief flooded her eyes when she glanced at him. "Halperts?"

He nodded. "ASAP."

Just getting out of the parking lot was tricky. The street-light beams were drastically dimmed by the snowfall; the windshield wipers could barely keep up.

She engaged the four wheel drive and despite jumping over a curb and grazing a stop sign, made it to the alley behind Halpert's store.

Their situation was grim at best, but he found it in him to grin over her driving. "Crash Craddock."

"At your service."

No apologies. He liked that, too.

"Sit. Rest," she ordered before jumping out of the truck, leaving it running with the heater on full blast. "I've got this."

He lost sight of her as she bucked the wind and rounded the cab toward the truck bed. He knew what she was after. This was no time for subtlety.

When she walked back to the front of the truck again, she had a tire iron in her hand. He couldn't hear the glass break above the wind, but he saw the moment she slammed the heavy iron into a window in the back of the store. Wasting no time, she used the tire iron to clear the glass shards from the frame, then hitched herself up and crawled through the open window.

He closed his eyes. Absorbed the warmth from the heater. Mentally assessed his injuries, then checked his face in the rear-view mirror. Damn. He looked like he'd been run through a meat grinder. His cheek and eye were both swollen but the cut had quit bleeding.

Remembering that he'd spotted some fast foot napkins in the glove box, he leaned forward and rummaged around until he found them, then made an attempt to clean some of the dried blood off of his face. Better but not great. The lump on the back of his head had given him a helluva a headache and though they hurt like the devil, he suspected his ribs were bruised but not cracked or broken.

Over all, he'd had worse. He'd been worse. But at the moment, he couldn't remember when.

A light came on in the back room, grabbing his attention. And a few minutes after that, Cara pushed the store's back door open and hurried back to the truck.

He opened the window so she could hand up two rifles, two 9mm S&W handguns, magazines for all four weapons and several boxes of ammunition.

He wanted to kiss her. But there wasn't time. "We could

use a GPS," he suggested as she climbed back up into the truck and behind the wheel.

She shot him a tight smile, unzipped her jacket and reached inside. "Will this do?"

A box with a brand new GPS landed on his lap.

He took stock of the ammo and magazines and stacked it on the console between them.

"Enough?" she asked.

Josh gave her a grim nod. "Depends on if we get there in time. Let's roll."

God's honest truth, he didn't know if they had enough of anything to face off with Matthews and his four goons. Another truth – it was going to have to be. Unless a miracle happened, they were on their own.

"You need medical attention," Cara said as she put the truck in gear and hit the gas.

"I'm fine. And there's no time. Just keep driving."

Because she knew he was right, she didn't say anything else about his condition. Instead, she called the sheriff's office, and set it to speaker phone.

She'd identified herself, reported the dead bodies, gave them the address, then related the situation.

"We've already gotten word of the planned attack from the governor's office," the dispatcher advised her.

Josh closed his eyes, knowing that meant RRA had been busy sounding the alarm about Matthews and his planned attack on the plant. It also meant that word had gone up to the White House and all of the Alphabet agencies. There was bound to be a lot of hand wringing going on at Capitol Hill and the Pentagon about now. They were aware that with this weather, and the deed going down right now in real time, that they couldn't do a thing but wait and hope that Josh and Cara could stop it.

"All of our deputies – on or off duty – have been called in to work because of the storm," the dispatcher said. "Unfortunately all units have already been dispatched to assist either stranded motorists or deal with accidents. We've got a ten car pile up on 380," she added sounding frazzled.

"All units have been alerted to leave any non-life-threatening call immediately and head to the Palo Plant. Unfortunately, all of them are at least an hour away – better make that two hours, provided they can even get there through the snow."

It was the same story after Cara hung up and called CRPD. All city units were already dispatched. Getting to the nuclear plant got top priority with the exception of life or death situations.

"Let's face it," Cara said grimly as she disconnected, "anyone stranded out in this weather – it's going to be life or death."

"If not for the weather," Josh said, "every branch of the military would have scrambled choppers and rained down ten kinds of hell already. Attack over before it even begins. But nothing can fly in this weather."

The closest National Guard Base was over an hour away in good weather conditions. The nearest Army installation was two hours. While they were preparing to deploy, they wouldn't get here in time. None of them would get here in time.

"I'm guessing that's why Matthews was insisting they move tonight. This blizzard is the best cover he could have possibly hoped for."

"I liked it better when we were on a recon mission," Josh said dead pan.

"Yeah," Cara agreed with a big sigh. "Life was simpler back then."

Josh smiled grimly. "Yeah. Way back six hours ago."

Way back six hours ago, they'd been on a flight in route to a simple recon mission that in all likelihood would result in a false lead. Now they were facing a nuclear disaster.

And it was up to the two of them to stop it.

Yeah. Way back six hours ago now seemed like a lifetime.

"I've got to get the laptop." Cara rounded a corner and headed for the motel. "RRA is sending a topography map, detailed security measures in place at the plant, checkpoints, plant blueprints, protocol. Anything that will either help us ward off or pinpoint any vulnerabilities Matthews may have found."

While Cara ran up the stairs for the laptop, Josh closed his eyes. Cleared his mind. Willed strength to return to his body. They had to succeed. They had to stop whatever plan Matthews' warped mind had devised. If they didn't ... well, if they didn't, not only were he and Cara dead, but the better part of the population of the Midwest could be obliterated along with them.

SHE CAME BACK with not only the laptop, but Tylenol, a few bottles of water, the pizza, and the stash of chocolate.

When Josh grinned at her, she gave him a pointed look. "Take the Tylenol. Drink the water and eat some pizza. Some chocolate wouldn't hurt either," she added.

When she glanced across the front seat at him and saw that he was still grinning, she put on her CO face. "Those are orders, Haskins. Your body needs protein and re-hydration. I need you alert and with the program."

"And you need chocolate." He managed another smile.

"Just hand me a piece of pizza. I could use the energy after dragging your car-sized carcass down those stairs."

"Pizza and the chocolate," he pointed out again.

"Damn straight."

THE GOING WAS SLOW. Maddening. Frustrating. Agonizingly slow.

"At this rate, we'll never catch them in time," Cara grumbled.

She felt defeated by their lack of progress. He could see that. He could feel it as deeply because he felt defeated too. They were literally plowing their own path with the nose of the truck. Only the fact that Matthews's truck, with a snow blade, had plowed through, by his estimation, no less than fifteen minutes ahead of them, kept them going forward. The wind blew with such force, though, that the path had already drifted closed in several stretches of the highway.

Josh glanced over at Cara, valiantly managing to keep the truck between the lines. She'd also managed to finish half a slice of pizza, down some water and was currently working on a chocolate bar when the laptop finally powered up.

The Files RRA sent were here. Waiting for them to load was like waiting for water to boil. But Cara had been right. He had started to feel a little better with some Tylenol, protein and water in him.

"Here we go," he said and opened up the first file.

He quickly scanned it then started paraphrasing the long reports aloud for her.

"The plant's located on five hundred acres on the west bank of the Cedar River. Two twelve foot high chain link fences with six feet separating them surround the complex of buildings that make up the plant. The fences are electronically monitored and there's a magnetic field running between them to detect any activity."

"Keep going," she said.

"Besides the fencing, after 9-11 watch towers were erected," he read on aloud. "Each one is manned with five guards. All towers monitor the grounds with cameras. And the entire perimeter is surrounded by lights. Both inside and outside the fences, it's lit up like a football field."

"What else?" Cara asked while they both thought through scenarios where a ground assault could be staged considering those barriers.

"A motor patrol with two guards armed with 9mm handguns constantly drives the parameter. Shift changes every hour. In the event of a security alert – which they're on right now – the guard houses at the checkpoint towers are equipped with shotguns and AR-15s."

"Back up a little," Cara said, her brows furrowed in thought. "How could motor patrols drive through this snow?"

Josh scanned the document. "They walk it. After their hour, the guards rotate to one of five positions. From fence patrol, to tower surveillance, to the camera room in the plant, to the guard house. Then they go to the entry site where they monitor the x-ray equipment for employees and approved individuals coming and going."

"So that makes what? Twenty five mobile guards on site at all times?" Cara calculated.

"Outside, right. Plus another twenty-five inside the plant who rotate from the door of one building to another."

"So – five against fifty? No way. Plus – there must be what? Another three hundred or so other employees on duty, right? Engineers. IT. Truck drivers. Clerical staff. Whatever. Matthews doesn't have the numbers. And the security is as tight as a tick."

"Doesn't mean it's impenetrable. It says here that in the early ninety's a guy drove his car past a checkpoint at the Three Mile Island Nuclear plant, broke through an entry gate and eventually crashed through a secure door and entered the reactor building. They didn't find him for over four hours. Turns out he had a history of mental illness but the point is, he could have been a terrorist armed with a bomb. One guy. Made it through."

"Fluke," she said. "No one knew he was coming. We know about these guys."

"Here's another little alarming tidbit for you," he said, reading further. "Our nuclear utility plants aren't required to protect against rocket-propelled grenades and sniper rifles with armor-piercing ammunition, weapons that any self-respecting terrorist is sure to have.

"So," he went on, "a commando type ground-based attack could potentially work. And if they went on to disable certain equipment, the result would be a reactor core meltdown or widespread dispersal of radio activity."

"Wow. I'm feeling better about this all the time."

He smiled, appreciating her gallows humor.

"Wait. How," she wanted to know before he began again, "can our nuclear power plants, with all the pools of used fuel stored there, be left so vulnerable? If these animals are successful, they could disable cooling systems, trigger meltdowns, and release massive amounts of radiation – like what happened at Chernobyl back in ... what?"

"The mid-eighties, I think," he supplied. "And don't forget Japan's Fukushima reactor during the tsunami. We'd all be in bad shape if they hadn't gotten that contained."

She signed heavily. He knew what she was thinking.

"We're going to get there, Cara. We're going to stop them."

She lifted a hand toward the windshield. The wipers worked valiantly to keep the glass clear of snow. "How? How are we possibly going to get there in time?"

"This isn't like you, Graves. You're not a pessimist."

She laughed. "Are you living in the same universe as I am? How can we-"

"We will. That's it. We have to. Now, what other questions do you have about the plant? We need to know the lay of the land once we get there."

She gathered herself and got back on board. "So, how many buildings are there in a nuclear power plant compound?"

"Now you're just testing me," Josh said but found what he was looking for. "Here it is. The containment building houses the reactor. Five foot thick walls reinforced with steel. Take a helluva a charge to breach that puppy."

He continued scanning for pertinent information. "There's an auxiliary reactor building - it stores emergency equipment and radio active liquids and gases. A turbine building, which obviously houses the turbine, generator, condenser, and the water systems. There's also an intake structure where water's pumped to and from the river – this is attached to a cooling tower.

"The last is a Diesel Generator building. It runs all the support systems - air, water, air conditioning, ventilation, etc. for inside the plant."

"And the most problematic or most vulnerable?"

"An attack on a reactor's spent fuel pool could be a good bet. The pools are less protected than the reactor core. The release of radioactivity from those pools could lead to exactly what we're trying to avoid. Thousands of near-term deaths and greater numbers of long-term fatalities."

Cara went quiet for a while, her hands tight on the steering wheel as they made slow forward progress. "Okay. So how are five men planning to breach what sounds to me like excellent exterior security then deal with fifty more interior guards all on red alert and waiting for them?"

He'd been giving that a lot of thought. "In this weather,

maybe fewer numbers are an advantage. If they time their breach of the fence when the guards are in mid-rotation, they could slip through, buzz under the magnetic shield, slip the other fence and head straight for the reactor. They could set charges all along the perimeter before even trying to enter the building. Before anyone could spot them or the charges."

"You're forgetting the lights around the perimeter. Even with the snow and the dark, it's possible the tower guards could spot them and take them out."

"Matthews isn't still alive because he's stupid. If there are blind spots, and that's a possibility, he's going to know where they are. Either that, or he knows where the electrical power grid is that runs the lights, magnetic field and guard towers and how to take it out. Create a blackout outside."

"So where's the power grid?"

He scanned more of the document. "Here it is. The grid that controls the exterior power – the towers, the lights, the magnetic field – everything outside – sets on a hill about a quarter mile away from the physical plant."

"Outside of the plant?"

"Right. If the power grid fails ... ," he scanned the document, "looks like normal protocol would be for the guards to stay on patrol, break out the long guns and wait while an engineer or two head out to check out the grid. In the meantime, they'll shut down the turbines, then the rest of the plant in an excess of caution."

Cara tapped her fingers on the steering wheel. "Matthews has to know how detailed and tight the security measures are. True, he docsn't know that security knows he's coming, but even at that, I'm not buying the possibility he could actually penetrate the complex and do any real damage."

Brows furrowed, she glanced at Haskins. "If that's the case, what does he have that we don't know about? What does he know that makes him think he can get in? And what does he think he can accomplish once he does?"

Before Josh could formulate an answer, the truck hit a slick spot on the road, fishtailed wildly, then plowed straight into a snowbank.

CHAPTER TEN

URI ALWAYS HIRED out to the highest bidder. Money played straight. Took all the guessing out of the game. There was never any question where loyalties lay. No religion in the mix to muddy the waters. No politics to corrupt – at least not on his end. And if there was on the other end? Well, that was their vice to deal with.

He dealt in results. Clean. Clear. Concise. Money made that happen when it passed into his hands. Someone wanted something done. They came to him. He had developed a reputation in the international community for anonymity, discretion, and results. His record stood on its own.

He always delivered. He never got caught.

He would deliver again tonight.

The truck lights blazed through the snow as they bounced along the road with Joe behind the wheel. Lack of visibility was a factor, however GPS took away the guesswork as the truck plowed forward toward their destination.

He didn't know the real names of the four men he'd subcontracted to assist in carrying out this job. He'd used them before. Found them able and discreet. That's all that mattered. Although, if he had to hazard a guess, he'd peg them as Syrian. For the sake of clarity, however, he'd dubbed them, Al, Joe, Ben, and Tom. Short, neat, and direct.

Likewise, these men didn't know his name. They knew him as Trent Matthews, one of many aliases he'd used over the years. In fact, he'd used aliases for so long that he rarely thought of his real name. No, Uri Avilov, was buried somewhere in the archived birth records for Gdov, Russia.

He'd been sixteen when he'd left the poverty and the boredom of the small village on the far western border of Russia. That was thirty-six years ago. He'd never looked back. He had no curiosity about his family. Peasants. All of them. He hated them because they were content to starve if that's what the government choose for them. Lemmings. Following each other to poverty and yes, starvation, and a life committed to nothing. They existed. And were content with it. It disgusted him.

Uri had not been content. And his drive had taken him to places he'd dreamed about as a boy in that God-forsaken corner of Russia. His drive had given him women more beautiful than goddesses. Money to feast on and luxurious hotels to live in by the ocean or the sea or wherever he chose to live between contracts.

So, no. He had no curiosity about Gdov or his family. Likewise, he had no curiosity about his stated objective. Had no idea why the target was an aging nuclear power plant in the middle of nowhere, United States of America. He hadn't asked. He'd had one long, intense meeting in Syria with Russian Spetsnaz operators defining his objective, learning about the new technology, calculating the risks.

Had he not thought he was capable of assembling a team to produce the desired results, he would not have signed the contract to perform the work. One did not fail when working with Spetsnaz. A professional 'acquaintance' had failed them once. How the Spetsnaz had dealt with them made the KGB look like puppy dogs.

Uri had confidence in his skills or he never would have agreed to carry out this job. In addition to every Western intelligence and special operations units looking for him, he did not wish to add Spetsnaz to the list.

The weather? The weather was actually a plus. He'd left no detail to chance. The large, club cab truck had duel wheels equipped with chains, four-wheel drive and a snow blade. No one else would be out in this direction in this weather this time of night. No one would anticipate an attack, in any event. Anyone who could have given him away was either dead or incapacitated.

He gave a fleeting thought to the man who was bound and gagged and passed out in Peet's apartment. It would be interesting to interrogate him when this was over. Establish if he would turn out to be a valuable commodity or merely another body bleeding out on the floor.

For now, he had a clear coast, as they said here. And he had fascinating weaponry – he was eager to employ it again after seeing it perform in the test firings. The technology would prove to be a game changer. And when he accomplished his objective tonight, it would alter the balance of international power forever.

Ultimately, that was his goal. Prove, in a real time situation, as opposed to simulation, the efficiency, effectiveness and the far reaching power to control destiny.

He checked the GPS. "Given our current progress, we're within thirty minutes of the power grid," he advised his crew. "Everyone is clear on their individual tasks."

It wasn't a question. It was an affirmation of the care he'd taken to ensure flawless execution.

First order was to take out the power grid, rendering the exterior perimeter dark and diverting the attention of the security guards away from the plant in anticipation of an assault.

Second order was to suit up and mask up to avoid any residual radioactive fallout, should an accident happen.

Third order was to set up on the north perimeter, just outside of the fence.

Finally, he would run through the meticulous checklist to arm the bomb, then dial in the pertinent specifications to deliver the entire payload. Mission accomplished in less than fifteen minutes.

They'd be back to the apartment, pick up their hostage and lay low in the house he'd rented in a small town twenty miles from Palo until the storm passed and the roads were cleared. They'd make the quick drive to Chicago, catch their international flights to parts unknown and collect the balance of his payment wired via a numbered Swiss account.

Then he'd sit back and watch the free world in the grip of a panic unlike any seen before.

"NOW WHAT?" Cara blew out a frustrated breath. They were stuck like super glue in a snowbank.

They'd rocked the truck back and forth from forward to reverse. Haskins had gotten out and pushed. They'd tried everything they could. Nothing worked.

"Now we improvise," Haskins said. He'd been filling both the rifle and handgun magazines with ammo while they'd driven and worked the problem of stopping Matthews. He tossed Cara half of the extra mags and gathered his rifle, the 9mm, and settled a pair of the NVG's with the IFR on his head.

"Grab your gear. And the GPS." He shoved open the passenger door and got out. "Don't forget your NVGs."

"And go where? Go how?" She had to yell to be heard above the wind as she joined him by the passenger door, snow slapping her face like icy sand. Like him, she loaded a magazine into the 9mm, settled the sling on the AR-15 over her shoulder, and fitted her pair of NGS on her head.

It was like being inside of a snow globe and being shaken by an angry giant. No matter that she was zipped up and covered in thermal snow gear, the combination of the wind and the cold penetrated like water into a leaky boat. Constant, persistent and inevitable.

Haskins lifted his chin toward a light that loomed high and ghostly about a block away and mostly obscured by the falling snow. "If I remember right, our new ride awaits us."

Then he started walking, plowing a path for both of them as he went.

"If we're where I think we are, I noticed it on our way in from the airport," he yelled over his shoulder as she worked to keep up with him. "Let's hope our luck holds and I'm right."

She was too cold to ask questions and too sure about Haskins' ingenuity to question him. He knew something she didn't and she was fine following him. He'd also regained his strength. Thank God.

As it turned out, her instincts were right about his. He led her to the open lot of a snowmobile dealership. Dozens of machines set in rows under the lights.

"Well, okay then," she said as they reached a row of sleds piled high with snow. "Which one?"

He quickly scanned the lot, then glanced toward the dealership building and the plate glass windows of the showroom.

"That one," he said and made a beeline toward the building.

Right on his heels, she peeked inside the large windows. A huge, shinning, white machine with black racing stripes and long, wide skis sat smack in the middle of the room, looking for all the world like a knight in shining armor. Or shining armor for a knight.

The nose of the machine was streamlined and sleek. The space age windshield gleamed under the showroom spotlight. Black grips fit the ends of the chrome handlebars. An array of dials and LED lights on the dashboard told her it was rich with any number of electronics. The sled was easily large enough for two and judging by the pair of astronaut class white helmets with full face shields setting on the leather seat, it was designed to carry two.

If it weren't for the urgency of their situation, she might have drooled a little over the sheer beauty and craftsmanship.

The sharp crack of two well placed rifle shots not only shattered the showroom glass, it broke her spell and drove her into action.

She helped Haskins clear the shards of glass projecting from the concrete windowsills, then climbed through the knee high window wall behind him and into the building.

Haskins flicked on a pen light, walked straight to the first closed office door and kicked it in. He came back out with a set of keys.

"They always save the best for the show room," he said, threw a leg over the bright white machine and inserted the key. The sled purred to life like a contented cat.

"Can you drive one of these things?" Cara asked, climbing on behind him.

"Guess we're going to find out."

Before engaging the gears, he made a quick study of the dash then grinned over his shoulder.

"Put your helmet on."

To do this, they both had to remove their NVG's which they re-affixed to the top of the helmets.

"Can you read me?"

Holy cow. The helmet was equipped with remote wireless head phones. "Loud and clear."

He pushed a few more buttons and she felt heat under her butt and the back of her thighs. Just when her face mask was beginning to cloud from the steam of her breath, Haskins pushed another button on the dash, and the fog cleared.

"Can it cook, too?" she asked as she settled herself in behind him.

"If it can, I'm going to marry it." He revved the engine with a turn of the handle bars. No contented cat this time. The engine came to life with the roar of a hungry tiger.

"There's a remote over there," he said pointing to the wall ahead of them.

She quickly jumped off, ran over and punched the remote. A large overhead door rolled up and open.

Haskins glanced over his shoulder as she swung a leg across the seat and settled in close behind him again. "You ready?"

After adjusting her rifle and making sure she was in control of her weapon, she wrapped her arms tightly around his waist. "Born ready."

He twisted the controls on the handle bars one more time then gave the machine a shot of fuel. They burst out of the open showroom like a comet, leaving a rooster tail spray of snow in their wake.

Apparently, he couldn't help himself. Haskins let out a whoop of pure joy as they raced out of the lot and onto the snow covered highway. "We're back in business. Nothing's going to slow this baby down."

Nothing but a squad of terrorists, bent on staging Armageddon, she thought grimly. But at least they had a fighting chance of catching up with them now.

She gripped him tighter and looked down the road ahead into the vast expanse of wind and white and cold.

As it turned out, they didn't need the GPS that Cara had lifted from Halpert's store. The machine, which Josh had begun to think of as Elizabeth the Great because of her intrepid, regal power, was equipped with a built in GPS.

Josh pulled a glove off with his teeth then punched in the address of the plant on the fly and their course was set. The only thing they had to worry about was the very real possibility of him steering the machine off the road and into a ditch. These country roads were narrow and with the ditches full of drifting snow, it was a very real possibility.

"What's our ETA?" Cara's voice floated in over the headset.

He checked the GPS. "Fifteen minutes at this speed."

"Can we make it faster?"

"Not if we want to get there alive. I'm already pushing it by relying completely on the GPS. Like flying a plane blind, no runway lights to help keep it between the lines."

"Alive...." she all but whispered.

"Yeah, alive."

"No... not arriving alive. Mother of God," Cara muttered.

"What? What's wrong?"

"I totally missed it. It ... it must have been the shock of seeing you there. In the apartment. Passed out and bleeding. I thought you might be dead."

"Missed what, for God's sake?" Josh repeated.

"One of the men asked Matthews what to do with you. He said ... Lord I can't believe I forgot this ... he said to leave you. That he'd deal with you when they got back. He suspected you might be spec ops ... or more. Thought maybe he might be able to use you for leverage in some way.

"Do you see it? What that means," she continued, her speech getting faster, "is that he intends to survive whatever blast he's planning on setting off. He plans to get out of this alive."

Josh tumbled her words around in his mind, refitting them until something made sense. Damn. She was right. "And that means he's never intended to breach the plant. He knows he'd be a dead man the minute he attempted to scale or dig under the fence."

"Exactly. If he died – which is not his MO - it would be pretty hard to extort the government to keep him from attacking another plant. Possibly one he's already compromised."

Except for the steady roar of the machine, silence filled their headsets.

"So what *is* his plan?" Cara finally asked. "If he knows he can't breach the compound ...."

"...Then he has a means of taking out the plant from outside the perimeter fence," Josh finished for her.

More silence, humming alongside the rumble of the machine.

"RPGs? Rockets?" Cara suggested after a long moment.

"I don't know of any rocket that's small enough to transport on a pickup that can also infiltrate five inches of steel and another five of concrete. And it would take a helluva a lot of RPGs."

"I think you just answered our question," Cara said, her voice tense.

"Something new," Josh said, his dread as heavy as Cara's. "He's got something we haven't seen yet. Some type of weapon RRA, NSA and the collective international defense agencies don't know about."

He swore under this breath.

"What?" she asked when he went silent.

"I was just thinking that this couldn't get much better. Two snow blind operatives hunting five terrorists – five that we know about - with an unidentified weapon designed to blow a nuclear plant that, if they're successful, would create hundreds of thousands, if not millions of human casualties. No pressure there."

He heard her heavy sigh through the headset. "Nope. No pressure at all."

CHAPTER ELEVEN

IT WAS JUST the two of them. That was their reality. All airports were closed. The highways were impassable. No cavalry was riding to their aid.

The weight of the responsibility bore down on Josh like a battleship.

It wasn't the first time they'd been forced to rely only on each other. On more than one operation, he and Cara had been separated from the rest of the unit and had improvised their way out of a dicey situation. Cara was a seasoned operative, cool and competent and fearless under fire.

And they hadn't come this far to fail.

"Hang on," he said over his shoulder. "Desperate times and all that." Then he gunned the machine and they flew down what was now a country road, per the GPS.

Talk about flying blind. The snow. The wind. The speed. The night. It was all working against them.

"Check your wrist screen. We should be close enough to catch their heat signatures soon." If he didn't hit a ditch or culvert or electrical pole before they got there.

"Already on. How close are we?"

Josh spared a glance at the GPS. "In another half mile, we'll be close enough to run over them."

He'd no more gotten the words out and the world sank out from beneath them. The big machine sailed down a hill nose first, flew in the air for several yards, then plowed through a series of snowdrifts like an ice breaker in the Arctic Sea.

He fought the handle bars to steady the machine. But gravity and velocity and the machine's weight got behind them and sucked them over the snow at warp speed.

They started to fishtail and tip sideways. He backed off the gas, slowing the treads, attempting to regain control.

"Lean!" he yelled as the right skis lifted off the ground.

She gripped him tighter around the waist and leaned hard right with him using their combined weight to counterbalance the heavy machine and keep it from tipping over.

"I'm losing her!" he yelled and backed off further on the gas.

Too far. The machine's treads stopped turning and the only thing propelling them forward then was gravity and velocity. Gravity lost the battle first.

"Tuck and roll!" Josh yelled just before the nose slammed deep into a monster snowbank, jerking them to a stop and hiking the rear of the machine into the air like a diving duck.

And they were airborne. Launched into the night like twin missiles.

* * *

Cara was Haskins' CO but she knew when to bow to circumstances and follow an order.

She tucked as she flew through the air. And when she hit the ground, she rolled and rolled until she crashed into a snow drift. For a disoriented moment, she lay there. Face first in the snow, every inch of her body screaming in pain.

Deep breath. Then a second before she could mentally

assess her condition. She carefully moved each limb. Her ankles, then her knees. Her wrists, her elbows. She felt each bruise but everything seemed to be in working order. Slowly, she pushed herself to her knees and tested her back and shoulders and neck. Again, everything worked, but her hip had taken the worst of the impact. She'd deal with that later.

She brushed the snow off her face shield, then looked around for Haskins. Squinting through the falling snow and brutal wind, she finally spotted him less than a yard away, making the same assessment of his injuries.

Thank God. He was alive. That was twice in one night she'd been afraid she'd lost him. Two times too many. She'd deal with that later, too. Right now she had to find her rifle and her NVGs and make sure everything was still working. That meant crawling around in the snow and digging for both.

Still on her hands and knees, she'd just started searching in a grid when Haskins grabbed her arm and set her upright.

He flipped up his face shield, then reached over and flipped hers up as well.

"Are you all right?"

She nodded. "You?"

"More or less." He wrapped an arm around her and pulled her tightly against him. And held on, both of them on their knees with the blizzard howling around them and the cold seeping into their bones. Only the adrenaline and their relief outdistanced the chill.

When he pulled back to search her face, the emotions she saw brought tears to her eyes.

"What? What's wrong? Are you sure you're okay?"

"Nothing can happen to you, Cara. As vital as this mission has become ..." he stopped, closed his eyes. "It's just, nothing can happen to you."

"Haskins..."

He cut her off with a gloved finger to her lips. "This is a helluva a fine time to realize that I'm in love with you. A helluva a time to face it."

She knelt in silent shock. The cold melted away, replaced by a deep yearning heat radiating directly from her heart.

"Haskins…" she tried again.

Again, he silenced her. "I love you, Cara. Deal with it."

And then he kissed her. Hard and deep and long.

She was still attempting to process his words when he broke the kiss, stood and held out a hand to help her to her feet.

"Your rifle," he said, handing it to her. "Found it when I crawled over here. What about the NVG's?"

It took a moment for her to find her voice. "Um… I … just found them."

"Let's hope everything still works. Come on. We might have to dig the sled out." Then he flipped down his face shield and started slogging through the drifts to the half buried machine.

I love you. Deal with it.

She didn't move. Couldn't move.

I love you. Deal with it.

Those six words swirled around her like the storm, dizzying and blinding and momentarily stranding her where she stood. Okay, granted, this was no time or place to discuss the repercussions of his declaration. And she probably should be angry that he'd blurted out *I love you,* kissed her, then left her there, reeling in the aftermath.

Yeah. She should be mad. One hundred percent of her focus at this moment should be concern about saving lives. They were possibly stranded in the middle of a killer storm and could freeze to death. If they managed to get moving again and the storm didn't kill them, then five terrorists hell bent on unleashing Armageddon probably would.

Yet when she pulled herself out of her trance and rushed to help him free the sled, she felt a sense of calm and comfort, almost as sweet as going home.

* * *

If not for the GPS and their NVG's, they would have overshot their target. As it was, they arrived later than Uri had hoped. But then, given this cursed Siberian-like weather, luck had played no small part in getting them here at all.

His plan rode on precision, not luck. So his mood was considerably dark as they drove along the perimeter of the plant, careful to stay one hundred yards away from the fencing.

They drove slowly, using an infrared camera to locate the heat signatures of the security guards patrolling the fence. Thanks to the IFR, Uri could spot five guards at any given time as they rotated along their watch. Thanks to Jeannie, he knew to the man, how many guards he was up against outside the buildings. Twenty-five. As long as their fuzzy red heat signatures moved with practiced precision along the fence line, he knew they had not been detected.

"Drive another quarter mile past the complex. That should get us to the power grid." He assumed there was a reason the grid had been built outside of the compound fence. Right now, he didn't question it as it made his plan that much more workable.

"Are you certain you can make it back to the coordinates on foot?" Uri asked Ben and Tom when they stopped and left the engine idling.

"We'll meet you at the launch position within twenty minutes of setting the charges," Tom assured him, pulling his white face mask over his hazmat suit.

The two men grabbed their AK-47's and slammed the rear doors behind them with a rush of arctic air and swirling snow.

With the wind howling this loud, there was no chance they'd be heard.

Uri and Joe waited, truck still idling as Tom and Ben opened the tail gate and rolled back the tarp covering the bomb far enough to get the C-4 and blasting caps they'd need to set the charges and blow the grid. A double rap on the truck box told Uri they had offloaded their weapons cache and were ready to get to work.

"Let's go."

Joe made a wide U-turn and headed back toward to the coordinates they'd established to set up the bomb.

Without asking for direction, Joe cut the headlights as an added precaution. Not that they expected the white truck could either be seen or heard in this storm, but because that was how he ran his operations. Nothing left to chance.

He didn't anticipate meeting up with the security, either, but he nodded in approval as he heard Al, alone in the back seat, making a final check on his weapons.

Uri had paid them for their professionalism. Appreciated that they worked together seamlessly as a team. Beyond that, he had no interest in their lives, in who they were, or where they were from.

Because he knew he could count on them, he'd been calm and in complete control from the moment he'd set things in motion. Of course Jeanne and the gamer boys had to be killed. He'd known that from the beginning. He'd lived this long because of his cardinal rule: Leave no witnesses. He'd only needed them to mine information.

So yes, all had gone smooth - only the unexpected 'guest' had added a wrinkle in his plans. He'd been quickly contained, however, and now the only reason his adrenaline was pumping was the anticipation.

Uri was eager to employ this new form of bomb. Eager to use his intellect and skills to carefully prepare it, set the velocity, the trajectory, and the coordinates to create maximum destruction. It wasn't that he relished killing. Killing was sometimes merely a necessary action to ensure success.

What he anticipated with such excitement was the completion of a perfect plan. The rush of racing against a clock, of the delicacy needed to handle such a dangerous weapon, the precision required to execute a mission faultlessly.

If all went well, Tom and Ben would arrive just as he and Joe, with Al providing over-watch, dialed in the coordinates and initiated the countdown. He anticipated fifteen minutes to make the bomb live. Only the severe weather conditions could slow things down. No matter. No one knew they were here. There was no need to hurry. This must be done right.

* * *

Josh couldn't fake it much longer. Neither could he put off telling Cara. She'd almost reached him and the machine that he hadn't been able to budge from the snowbank.

Telling her that he loved her had been enough of a shock. He still wasn't sure if she'd been pleased or ticked off by his declaration. But he knew for certain that she wasn't going to like his next one.

"What do you want me to do?" she asked as she joined him by the machine.

He flipped up his face-shield. "Well, right now, I'd like you to put my shoulder back in place."

Her face-shield flew up. Her eyes widened in concern as he lifted his right hand and cupped his dislocated shoulder.

"Oh, my God! How bad is the pain?"

"One to ten, I'd give it a twenty." Still he tried not to let her see how much pain he was really in.

He'd been gritting his teeth and hoping he'd been wrong. He wasn't. When he'd flown off the machine, he'd landed with the brunt of his weight on his left shoulder. Adrenaline had been pumping hard and fast, masking most of the pain. The adrenaline burst had since let down and now he had no question. He couldn't go on until it was back in place. Fast. Passing out was becoming a real possibility.

"Are you sure? Could it be broken?" Cara asked, her concern showing in her eyes.

"Been here before. Absolutely sure."

He'd been a kid the first time he'd dislocated his shoulder. He'd been wrestling with his brother and things had gotten out of hand – as they usually did. Of course they were home alone. Luckily, their next-door neighbor – a nurse – had heard his screams and rushed over to see what was wrong. When he wouldn't let her take him to the hospital because he knew his mom and dad would be angry, she'd reluctantly - sending prayers skyward, and begging for guidance - reduced the dislocation then made him a makeshift sling out of a dish-towel. Problem solved.

He'd been deployed with his Special Forces unit in Iraq the next time it had gone out. He and the guys had been playing basketball against another squad during a rare slot of down time.

Emotions in combat ran from high to low in a heartbeat. They were either bored out of their minds or fighting for their lives. It made for a lot of steam that needed to be let off. And that made for a lot of competitive spirit even in little pick-up basketball games. Often there was enough contact that it could have been a football game. *Boys will be boys.* Which is how he'd been on the receiving end of a blind-sided shove and, taken by surprise, hadn't been able to check his fall.

He'd landed hard on his shoulder. Ironically, the guy who had blind-sided him was a doctor. He'd quickly hauled him off to x-ray in the hospital tent, reduced the shoulder then supplied him with an order for thirty days of light duty and enough pain medication to see him through it. It had been hard to be mad at him after that.

Now here he was again. The only reason to be thankful for the other two dislocations was that he had a pretty good idea of how to fix this one.

"What do I do?"

If her face hadn't shown her worry, her voice did. But he could see in her eyes that she was also determined to see this through.

"I need to be flat on my back."

Snow or no snow, cold or no cold, the ground was the only flat surface.

He lay down then biting back a groan, stretched his injured arm away from his body at a 90-degree angle.

Despite the bitter cold, sweat broke out on his forehead. His stomach roiled. And he prayed to God that he stayed conscious.

"Sit down beside me and position your feet against my side. That's going to give you additional leverage.

"Good," he said as she eased down in the snow beside him and placed her feet against his rib cage.

Now came the really rough part. "When I say go, you need to firmly grab my hand or wrist – whatever you can get the best grip on - and slowly, but firmly, pull on my arm. That's going to create traction."

"And it's going to hurt you."

"Yeah. But it'll be over fast. If I pass out, slap some snow on my face to bring me around."

"Oh, God." She hung her head. "You know you need a doctor to do this. X-rays."

"It'll be fine. And it's not like we have any options. Again, when I say go, pull my arm. So you can visualize it, this angle allows the head of the humerus to slide under the bone of my shoulder blade and back into its socket. Piece of cake."

"For who? Certainly not for you. And not for me either. I'm afraid of hurting you more."

"You've got this, Cara. I need you to have this. Okay?"

She sucked in a determined breath. Let it out. "Okay. I'm ready. Say when."

He closed his eyes. Braced himself. "When."

CHAPTER TWELVE

URI COULDN'T HELP but be impressed by American ingenuity. He was particularly enamored by their automobile and truck industry. It took a strong, heavy duty pickup to hold his particular payload. It had been important that an American truck – this one a new Chevy 3500, with dual tires – was used for the mission for a number of reasons.

It seemed that almost everyone in the Midwest of the United States drove a pickup truck. They weren't reserved for ranchers and farmers anymore. He hadn't wanted to draw attention with a cargo truck. It would stand out too much. Cause questions. This truck only stood out because it was beautifully crafted. Not to mention, it handled quite well in the snow.

Additionally, the truck bed was a full twenty-two inches deep, eight feet long and could carry close to six thousand pounds. More than adequate to transport his client's cutting edge bomb.

The weapon was capable of producing a super heated jet of plasma able to burn through the building housing the nuclear reactor from up to one hundred yards away. He only needed fifty yards, doubling his odds of penetrating the wall constructed of five feet of steel and five feet of reinforced concrete.

The bomb was actually quite inventive. The Russian Spetsnaz delegation that had met with him in Syria had been very enamored with their weapon and the engineers who had built it. They had accomplished what no one else had managed to do: engineer a bomb that had been reduced to a size compact enough to carry and deliver on the ground.

How they had done it, he didn't know. But he'd bombed enough targets to know that this bomb was brilliant and perhaps one hundred percent more powerful than any he'd ever used before.

The twenty-four and a half inches of thick, stainless pipe weighed in at four hundred pounds. Amazingly it was only seven feet long.

They had invented a new kind of plastic explosive – four hundred fifty pounds worth. With the additional bracing and copper plating, the total weight was right around four thousand pounds.

Two tons. They'd compacted a bunker buster bomb that previously had to be transported and dropped from a massive bomber down to approximately two tons. Again. Brilliant. And the balance of world power would soon change because of it.

What was even more noteworthy was that they'd morphed the mounting for the bomb from a World War II era Polish MPB anti-tank mine so it could be mounted horizontally in an adjustable frame. This allowed it to be launched from the back of a truck or from the ground. Previously unheard of.

Uri had no idea how the Spetsnaz had smuggled it into the States. But then it was not known how often and how large numbers of illegal products managed to escape detection at the massive US sea ports. The fact that over eleven million maritime containers arrived in those ports every year definitely played a hand in it. That and the money that changed hands to ensure that the container holding the bomb had been overlooked.

He only knew that the bomb had been waiting for him at the specified warehouse in California, where he'd picked it up over four months ago and driven across country with it. More money had apparently greased the necessary palms to get it there.

"Stop here," he ordered Joe.

Snow flew in the window as he lowered it. Uri angled the infrared camera around the immediate area, consulted with the GPS, and finally nodded. "This will do. Turn the truck around so the tailgate is facing the plant."

"Keep it running?" Jo asked, maneuvering in reverse until he had the truck in position.

"Yes. This blizzard may require that we have to take a break from setting up to get warm. Frozen fingers are clumsy and clumsy fingers make mistakes."

Uri couldn't afford any mistakes. Not at this juncture. With luck, he'd have the bomb system set up, calibrated, engaged and ready to remote detonate within minutes.

They'd ex-filtrate the target sight, make sure they were at least ten miles away and rely on a timer to detonate.

In the short term, anyone within a mile of the blast would be dead on impact. In the long term, hundreds of thousands would die as the radioactive clouds thickened the atmosphere like fog.

He would be alive – and millions of US dollars richer.

INSIDE HIS HEAD, Josh screamed like a little girl. That's what he'd wanted to do. Scream like bloody hell. For Cara's sake, he kept it down to an animal groan and figured he'd cracked at least two teeth because he'd clenched so hard.

"You got it," he managed on a grunt of exquisite pain when she let back on the tension.

"Thanks, God." She looked as relieved as he felt. "Are you okay? You look gray."

"Yeah," he said, attempting to sit up, but fell back down with another groan. "Help me up."

No time. There was no time. And while the pain in his shoulder had ratcheted down by several degrees, it still hurt like a bitch. He'd started to shiver. And hoped he wasn't going into shock. Regardless, he needed to get warm. No doubt, so did Cara.

"That arm should be in a sling."

Yeah. That wasn't going to happen. "Help me get this machine free. You climb on and start her up. I'll lean on the front end."

She gave him a look. One that said she didn't like this, but that she knew they had no other choice. She crawled onto the sled, checked out the dash to familiarize herself with the controls, then cranked the key.

Josh held his breath … until the engine revved, sounding up fit and fine. *Thank you, God.*

"Now slip it in reverse." And thank God for reverse or they'd really be in trouble. Once upon a time snowmobiles had only one gear. Forward. *Let's hear it for progress.*

It took a little rocking back and forth to free the sled but after a few minutes of manipulating, praying, and swearing, the cleated tracks finally gripped and Cara backed clear of the deep drift. The woman could do anything.

"We've lost too much time," he said straddling the seat behind her and leaning into her for warmth.

"I'm driving?" Both surprise and excitement accented her voice.

"Up to it?"

"Oh, hell, yeah."

She made sure her NVG's and IFR were working, that the sled's GPS was still on target, and flipped down her face shield. "Hang on."

Despite his screaming shoulder, and the chills racking his body, he chuckled when she hauled out of there like their tail was on fire.

Soon, blessed heat radiated from the seat through his snow pants and started warming the back of his legs as they flew along. The warmth was a lifesaver as it crept into his body, eventually warming his bones. He closed his eyes and leaned his head against her shoulder, putting all of his trust in her.

He needed this short respite. Had trained his mind to relax and gather as much rest and strength as possible in any number of situations. Power naps. They saved the free world. The one thing he needed above all else right now was to have his batteries recharged and loaded back up with a little energy. Between the beating Matthews and his goons had dished out and the pain ripping through his shoulder, he was pretty much tapped out.

He fell asleep — although some would categorize it as passed out — to the warmth of the heated seat, the purr of the engine and the feel of his chest pressed against Cara's back.

"HASKINS."

Josh heard his name through a fog. Decided he'd imagined it and drifted back to sleep.

"Haskins! Are you with me back there?"

No mistaking it. *That* was real. *That* was Cara Graves' commanding officer voice.

"Yes, sir," he responded, lifting his head and shaking out the cobwebs. "I'm with you. How long was I out?"

"Less than five minutes. Look. Haskins. You need to be up front with me here. Lord knows you've been beat up enough today that you should be in a hospital bed, not out in this blizzard on a snowmobile. Definitely not taking on Matthews and his crew. So if you're not up to this, I need to know. And I need to know now."

"I'm good," he said, then made the mistake of testing his mobility. Pain shot through his shoulder, searing down to his hand. Sharp, burning, unbelievable pain. He sucked it up. He would not pass out. He could do this. He would do this. She needed him. A lot of people needed him to be on his game.

"So help me, God. If you get killed because you weren't physically capable of dealing with these miscreants, I'll never forgive you."

"Never's a long time. But just for you, I'm not getting killed, okay? We have unfinished business after we deal with Matthews and I plan to be around to finish it."

She hesitated a moment. Must have decided to let that dog lie for a while longer. "Start checking your wrist cam then," she said in her best CO voice. "GPS says we should be almost on top of the plant."

She cut the headlight and backed off on the throttle which allowed Josh to let go of her and lift his right arm to position and check his IFR wrist camera.

Slowly and methodically, he scanned the frozen landscape. The wind was so strong in this open stretch of land that it blew the snow sideways. He could have been on top of Matthews' truck and not known it if he'd been counting on his vision alone. And only if this IFR camera worked the way the boys at R & D promised, would he be able to pick up a heat signature in this blizzard.

Cara let the snowmobile creep along barely above idle. The longer they were at it, the more frustrated he became. Then he saw it.

"Stop," he said abruptly. "I think I caught a ghost of a heat signature."

She throttled back to a stop.

He zeroed in on the spot, squinting to see, then jolted and swore when a blast exploded through the storm and rumbled above the snowmobile's engine.

The sky lit up like a volcano in the distance. Another blast ripped into the night followed by five more successive explosions.

"Holy hell!" Cara swore. "What the ..."

"They just took out the power grid." Josh watched the ghostly yellowish glow burn through the low cloud cover and falling snow.

"They didn't go easy on the explosives."

The scene was eerily beautiful as plumes of white and gray and black clouds billowed up and above the fire that burned at least forty feet in the air. The huge flames licked at the darkness and turned it light.

"Haskins," she said abruptly. "Look at your wrist cam. See if you see what I'm seeing."

He looked away from the blaze and angled his wrist back to the right, where he thought he'd seen a signature before. After several moments, he picked it up again. Make that four heat signatures.

"I've only got four," Cara told him. "One of them is much larger than the other three and stationary."

"That's what I'm seeing. The big one must be the truck. The engine's still hot or it's still running. The other three are men."

"There were five of them. Where are the other two?"

"They must have split up. Two of them must have torched the power grid and are on their way back here."

"They could have rigged those explosions at the grid to remotely detonate. We need to be careful. The other two may be just out of camera range."

"I don't think so," Josh said, processing the time and the space they'd covered. "They didn't have time to set up there then set up here. I know we had a delay or two, but they didn't get here that long before we did. At least not far enough ahead that they could have set the explosion at the grid then driven back over here and set up. They weren't making the time we were on this sled."

"Okay. I can see that," Cara agreed. "So, they split up. But why?"

They thought in silence, watching the small red figures move around approximately thirty yards away. Under normal circumstances, he and Cara would have been spotted from this close proximity. The snowmobile would have been heard. But the snow blocked visibility. The wind blew against them, carrying any sound they made away.

And the light from the explosion at the power grid didn't penetrate this far to illuminate them. They were well hidden in the dark and the blizzard.

"Maybe because of what you just said," Cara said thoughtfully. "What if they were trying to save time? What if they blew the grid as a diversion for the plant guards so the other three could have a little extra time setting up here to do their real damage?"

"That's why you're the boss," Josh said. "You've got all the right questions."

"That would surely mean that Matthews is here, not at the grid, right? He's in control and he'd want to be in control of blowing the plant."

She was spot on again. Which meant Matthews had been here a while. He could be set and ready to go or very close to it.

They were running out of time.

"We've got to move." Cradling his bad arm, Josh dismounted.

Cara cut the engine and joined him, slinging her rifle over her shoulder and digging the 9mm out of her pant leg pocket.

She stopped him with a hand on his arm. "Are you absolutely sure you're physically able to do this?"

"As sure as I am that I'd like to be on a beach in Fiji right about now," he lied.

In truth, the only thing he was sure about was that he was not going to let her deal with these bastards on her own. As sure as he was that they were going to stop a national tragedy. As sure as he was that he'd die before he'd he let anything happen to her.

Gritting back the pain, he tucked the butt of his rifle between his good arm and his side and thought back to all those drills where he and the guys had practiced shooting from the hip in preparation for just this type of situation; an injured arm, an arm full of a rescued hostage, or a payload of enemy intelligence while under fire and running for their lives towards the ex filtration site.

Looked like tonight was the night he was going to get to test himself – in more than one way.

It was show time. And they were going to bring Matthews down or die trying.

CHAPTER THIRTEEN

AFTER THE THREE of them had suited up, Joe and Al shoveled an area five feet by seven feet to accommodate the bomb. It took the three of them to roll back the cover on the truck bed that hid the bomb, then to slide the seven foot ramp out from under the suspension platform cradling it.

Once the ramp was lined up with the steel rails, the two ton plus bomb was mobile. A simple system of ropes and pulleys effectively made the weight manageable and they slid the bomb carefully down and out of the truck bed then settled it on the ground.

Now that it was securely on terra firma, the next order of business was to erect a polar tent over it.

The three of them wrestled against the wind to get the parachute fabric into place but once the four corners were staked into the frozen ground, it popped up over them and the bomb and held strong.

"You're on watch," Uri ordered Al, moving on to the next phase of the set up.

Al gave him a clipped nod and walked back to the idling

truck for his rifle, then assumed an over-watch position at the front of the truck.

"Get our rifles," Uri ordered Joe and turned to the bomb.

It wasn't that he thought they'd need them but he was never comfortable on a job unless he was armed.

While security at these interior power plants was plentiful and well trained, the possibility that more than a handful of the guards had ever seen combat or were, in anyway, prepared mentally to withstand a commando style attack were pretty slim. Like Jeannie. She was a middle-aged woman who needed a job and managed to pass all of the training requirements without any law enforcement or military experience. The jobs were tedious and difficult with long hours. But the wages paid the bills and that was the bottom line for Jeannie. Probably, it was the bottom line for many of the security guards.

They were well trained and dedicated ... but experienced warriors? No.

Even if security was wise enough to figure out that when the power grid blew the blast was a diversion and sent a foot patrol looking for them, Uri planned to be finished setting up and on the way out before they ever got a read on his location, let alone find him. And if, on the off chance they did, Al would take them out.

He glanced at his watch. Ben and Tom should be setting the blasts off any moment now.

Uri had given Joe the instructions on the trigger mechanism's final assembly ahead of time so he could study them and assist with arming the bomb.

He looked over his shoulder as Joe slipped back inside the tent with the rifles, zipping up behind him, shutting out the brunt of the blizzard. The wind assaulted the lightweight parachute fabric, punching it from all directions as it swirled across the flat landscape, but the tent held firm. So did the cold.

Now that Joe was back, they went to work immediately.

Joe held a battery powered light over the work area. The assembly was precise, delicate work. Despite the cold, sweat beaded on Uri's brow as Joe fed him step by step directions, each step more sensitive than the one before it. One mistake at this juncture – one minute misstep - and he wouldn't live to see the reports on the international news channels.

And oh, how he relished those reports.

The president of the United States has placed the entire nation on red alert after an as yet unidentified person or persons succeeded in breaching the security of a nuclear energy plant housed in a Midwestern state and launching a bomb that badly compromised the plant, releasing toxic radioactive waste into the environment. Casualties from the force of the blast are reported to be in the thousands. The residual fallout from the explosion of the heavily damaged main reactor, however, has spread to vast portions of surrounding states ensuring more death and devastation that will elevate the long term fatality numbers into the millions.

He sat back on his heels. Drew a steadying breath. He was getting ahead of himself. They had to finish the job, set the timer and get out of there without killing themselves or being discovered. While he anticipated little if any percentage of discovery, he knew that plans failed when every angle wasn't covered.

Killing themselves, however, had always been a very good possibility.

For now, they were ahead of the game.

He tightened the final screw and nodded at Joe. "Good work."

The bomb was now fully assembled. The nuclear reactor building was dialed in as the designated target of the hot plasma jet. To minimize the danger of something going wrong, he'd taken the time to assemble the timer mechanism before they'd ever left for the plant. And was damn glad he had. The cold remained brutal. He was ready to get out of it.

But he still had to attach the detonator and the timer to the bomb then set it.

On a deep breath, he meticulously inserted two blasting caps wired in parallel into the plastic explosives. Once he was satisfied with their placement, he attached the other end of the wires into the timer.

One more step. The most dangerous one.

They'd been out in the cold working for at least twenty minutes. His fingers were starting to stiffen up.

He flexed them several times. Cupped them together and warmed them with his breath.

"Do you need to go back to the truck to warm up?"

Uri glanced at Joe, considered it for a moment, wondered if Joe was really concerned about him getting warm, or about getting blown up. He shook his head. "Less than a minute and I'm done. The only step left is powering up the timer."

That was the most dangerous part of assembling a bomb - powering up the timer. A missed solder joint, a wire attached to the wrong part of the circuit board - and he'd be dead in milliseconds.

On a bracing breath, he picked up the battery in one hand and the connector in the other. Just then an explosion boomed, followed by another, then another, and the earth rumbled beneath his feet.

His heart lurched and he fought to steady both hands

He'd been concentrating so hard that it took a millisecond for his brain to connect the dots. Tom and Ben had just blown the power grid.

Soon all personnel inside or out of the complex would be focused on the explosion. The exterior lights of the complex were out. The magnetic field was down. The tower had no power to run their spotlights or cameras. They had to be spooked.

He allowed himself a smile. "We won't have to worry about patriotic security guards stumbling in our direction now. Their attention is going to be on the grid for the immediate future."

Gathering himself again, he focused, once more, on the task at hand. Very carefully, he connected the battery and the timer.

This was it. His next move could be the difference between mission accomplished and his own death — the ultimate failure.

Fighting an adrenaline rush of anxiety, he steadied his breath, held it … then flipped the switch to activate the timer.

And he was still alive.

So was the bomb. Very alive and ready to fire.

He let out a long, relieved breath, and watched as the timer started counting down.

* * *

Belly crawling toward Matthews and his men was not a possibility. Thankful that the wind actually buffeted against him and helped keep him upright, Josh stooped low, struggling through thigh deep snow and deeper drifts. While he repeatedly checked his wrist camera to keep those three heat signatures in sight, it took most of his concentration to stay on his feet. If he went down on his shoulder, he couldn't guarantee that he wouldn't pass out. And be no good to anyone.

Cara insisted on staying beside him, refusing to pull ahead.

"Together," she said before they started the fifty yard approach toward one of the most critical targets they'd ever face. Other than the heat signature from the truck and the three smaller signatures indicating three men, they didn't know what they were walking into.

It didn't matter. Matthews had to be stopped.

From that moment on it was about one thing: pushing on to neutralize the threat – no matter what the cost – before Matthews blew the reactor to kingdom come.

Cara touched her hand to his arm. Gave him the sign to stop. He needed a short break to catch his breath. He suspected that she did, too. They were both winded. His lungs burned from sucking in frigid air as they battled the deep snow and wind.

They were within ten yards of their target and could actually make out a shadow of the truck but the snow flew so hard and thick he still couldn't see images without the infrared camera. The constant assault of snow and cold burned against his face.

Cara braced her back against the lashing snow then knelt directly in front of him so they could communicate easier above the constant roar of the wind.

"The heat signatures. They couldn't be anyone but Matthews and his men, agreed? The security guards maintain a tight line inside the perimeter."

Josh nodded. Only someone up to no good would be out in this weather, at a nuclear power plant, with an explosion blasting off nearby. "It's Matthews. No worry about taking out the wrong targets."

"Also agreed that the IFR indicates we've got one man on guard in front of the truck and two others huddled over something inside what ... a tent? At least I think I can make out a tent."

"It's a bomb," Josh said. "They're huddled over a bomb. And yes. One guarding. The other two working on it."

The IFR camera couldn't find signals from cold steel and explosives, but judging by the way the two red heat signatures were crouched close and moving slowly and methodically indicated they were setting something up.

"A bomb," Cara agreed. "Which could already be live. We've got to take them out before they finish what they're doing."

Left unsaid was how careful they'd have to be. They could detonate the bomb if they misfired.

Yeah. That was a bit of a dicey problem. "They planned on coming back to get me, remember? That means they'll have to remote detonate or have a timer in play. And that means they have to get in that truck and drive off. Which means they'll be away from the bomb at some point and we can take clear shots."

While he couldn't see much in the cold and snow, he could read body language.

"What?" he asked, suddenly feeling like a shoe the size of a boat was about to fall.

"RRA wants Matthews alive if possible."

It was a boat all right. A battleship.

He searched her eyes. Shook his head. Of course they did. They'd want to mine him for information about all the other bombings and find out who he works for.

Josh swore under his breath. "Well. That ups the OMG level by a few decibels."

"Yeah. So ... what do you think?"

"I think we should take out the bastard and his minions without so much as a hint that they have an option of surrender."

"Agreed. But..."

"But we have our orders. I know. How do you want to do this?"

"Got to figure that the one guarding is one of his men," she said.

Again Josh agreed. "Matthews is the boss. He'd definitely be in the tent."

"I'll take the guard out first," Cara said. "Wait until someone comes looking for him. That man will not be Matthews."

"Right. Matthews would send someone to check. He wouldn't do it himself. Problem of ID solved."

"Now if they just cooperate and give me a good shot."

He gave her a hard look. "Be careful."

She nodded, then every inch the warrior, advanced forward on her knees until she was a yard or two closer. Close enough to make out the guard's silhouette through the wild vortex of snow whipping all around them. She dropped to her stomach and dug her elbows into the snow.

Josh watched as she carefully sited down the length of her rifle, knowing that when she was satisfied she could make a clean shot, she'd take it.

It was mechanical for a soldier. It was a job that needed to be done. The mind, the heart, the soul compartmentalized until only the soldier remained. Only survival – hers, his, but overarching it all was the survival of their country.

He held his breath along with her. Knew the toll each kill took on her and every man or woman protecting their home, their city, their country. Just like he knew this one would visit in the night in some far distant dream and she would weep. For his soul. For hers.

This was not the night. This night, she'd do her sworn duty.

He watched her shoulders rise with a deep inhale, then slowly fall on a steady exhale. And she squeezed the trigger.

Josh saw the guard jerk, then fall.

Then he watched intently for the other two men to react to the shot. Training his rifle toward the tent, he tried to make himself smaller so he wouldn't be spotted.

There was no need to worry. One of the heat signatures moved rapidly and rushed to where the guard had been standing.

Cara took him out, too. Clean and neat. Without hesitation. Doing her job.

Heartbeat escalating with adrenaline, and fighting the pain, Josh averted his attention back to his IFR wrist cam. The remaining figure stood frozen inside the tent before ducking down low, realizing he may also be in the cross hairs of a rifle.

Matthews.

They needed to get to him before he engaged whatever mechanism he'd used to start the countdown process to detonate the bomb.

Cara came to the same conclusion at the same time as he did. She had the lead on him when he stood and started running as fast as he could through the drifts. It wasn't long before adrenaline took over and he overtook her.

Matthews had ducked down to all fours, a rifle in hand, and was scrambling out of the tent toward the driver's side of the truck.

"Matthews!" Josh yelled, the butt end of his weapon bolstered against his hip, his finger on the trigger. "Stop or you're dead."

At that very instant, Josh heard shots behind him. Cara dropped to her belly and fired in the direction of the snowmobile.

They had company. The two missing men had returned from blowing up the power grid and were laying down fire.

"You okay?" he yelled, fighting the howling wind.

"Get Matthews!" she yelled back and set the AR-15 to its task, popping off three round bursts at the two terrorists.

Matthews took advantage of the temporary distraction to shoulder his rifle and fire at Josh, and 'take him alive' got lost in the volley of shots blasting between them through the swirling snow.

His heart beat so fast it felt as though his entire body was turbo charged. He didn't feel pain now. He felt nothing but duty. Was fueled by muscle memory and adrenaline.

Matthews fired again. Josh returned fire. The brittle cold air rang with the sound of automatic weapon fire coming in bursts, then singles, then bursts again.

Suddenly, Matthew's weapon fell silent.

Josh took that chance to glance in Cara's direction. She was on her feet, creeping toward him. Thank, God. She was all right. And apparently, she'd eliminated the other two threats.

"Matthews?" she asked as she sank down in the snow beside him.

"Quiet. Could be hit. Could be playing possum. I need a new mag," he said, his shoulder making it impossible to change out his empty one for a full one.

She quickly reloaded the rifle for him then flipped her free hand in a circular motion, indicating she was going to circle around the back of the truck.

Josh nodded and when she was out of sight, fired off a few rounds in Matthew's direction just to see if he could goad him into firing again.

Again silence, then Cara's head popped up from behind the hood of the truck.

"He's down."

"Alive?" Josh yelled as he rose.

"RRA will be happy to know that you didn't kill him."

Josh didn't wait to find out how badly Matthews was injured. Out of breath, and caught off guard by a sudden light-headedness, he stumbled toward the tent and looked inside.

"Ceee-rist."

Matthews and his thugs may be out of commission, but they were a long way from being out of the woods.

It was a bomb all right. A big mother. And not just a bomb. It was a bomb he didn't recognize. A bomb that he had no doubt could change the world as they knew it.

And it was, upon closer inspection, a bomb that was rigged with a digital timer set to detonate in four minutes, twenty seconds and counting.

He stuck his head outside of the tent. "Cara! Get Matthews over here. Now!"

Then he waited, studying the timer and detonator, trying to figure out if there was any way to disarm the bomb without setting it off.

He saw nothing. Nothing.

They would need Matthews to disarm it for them.

Feeling dizzy again, he dropped to his knees, cradling his bad arm against his ribs, attempting to ease some of the pain. What seemed like hours but was less than thirty seconds from when he'd yelled for her, Cara shoved Matthews inside the tent ahead of her.

She'd bound his arms behind his back with flex cuffs. Blood stained his white snow pants high on the outside of his thigh, above his knee.

Matthews glared at him as recognition dawned. "Should have killed you when I had the chance."

"Disengage it," Josh ordered him.

Matthews, clearly in pain, still smiled. "I don't think so."

Josh glanced back at the timer. Had to blink to get it in focus. Three minutes and five seconds.

Josh glanced at Cara, shook his head, indicating they were running out of time.

"You didn't plan to die here, Matthews," Cara reminded him. "But you're going to if you don't disengage that timer."

Matthews shrugged but Josh could see he was sweating from fear.

"If we leave now, we'll just make it out of the blast area when it blows," Matthews said, his voice tempered with pain.

"But we're not leaving. Now disarm it you son of a bitch!" Josh yelled.

It was in that moment that Josh could see the transition in Matthews's eyes. He'd resigned himself. He'd accepted that he was going to die.

He was not going to help them.

Josh breathed deep. Glanced at the fuzzy timer again. One minute fifty-nine seconds.

He had to do something.

"Give me your 9mm," Josh told Cara as he set his rifle down.

She handed over her handgun. "What are you going to do?"

"Short of wishing I'd taken a class in disarming bombs, I'm going to punt."

"You're going to ... shoot it?"

He carefully moved the timer as far away from the bomb as the wires allowed. A whole six inches.

"Wouldn't it be worth trying to cut the wires?" Cara asked, with a tension he'd never heard in her voice before.

If he bungled this, she was going to die. They were all going to die.

"Cutting wires is for the pros. I'll ... kill us all for sure."

He glanced at the timer again. Fifty-five seconds and ticking.

He looked at Cara where she still held Matthews at gunpoint just inside the tent. Her eyes were wide, her breathing fast and shallow. She was terrified but she stood her ground.

"Heard this from a bomb tech one night in Iraq. Said if

you were ever faced with a ..." he had to pause to catch his breath. "... with a bomb set to detonate by timer, shoot the timer full of buckshot. If you don't have a shotgun, the next best ... best thing is a 9mm."

Thirty-six seconds and counting.

"Will it work?"

He looked from her beautiful face back down at the timer with bleary eyes.

"Sure hope ... so," he said. "Said he ... always loaded the last of the magazine ... with heavy duty rounds. Made it like sub-machine ammo ... made it able to punch through walls ... cars and whatever got in the way.

"Hope you loaded heavy enough, Cara."

"Josh. Just do it!" Cara urged as the timer ticked down to nineteen seconds.

"My buddy said to ... shoot the box with all the wires coming out of it. Sound right Matthews, or whatever your name is?"

What was wrong with him? Everything was fading in and out. "The plan is to ... to disrupt the firing circuit and damage the explosive matrix, and voila, dead bomb."

"Josh," Cara's voice wavered, pleading, almost a whisper. "Please. Just shoot it."

He glanced at her again. "Remember what I said. Take that with you if we go."

"I love you, too," she whispered, her eyes brimming with tears that trickled down her half frozen cheeks.

Five seconds.

He dropped to his knees and with shaking hands, aimed the 9mm directly at the center of the timer and leaned on the trigger.

CHAPTER FOURTEEN

Cara closed her eyes. Her heart slammed inside of her chest. Shoot a timer attached to a bomb?

She knew her remaining moments on earth could be numbered. Knew she might never discover what could have been with her and Haskins. Regretted every second that they had denied their love for so long.

"Shoot it! Just shoot it!," she whispered just before rapid fire blasts from the 9mm emptied into the timer and stopped her heart.

The echoing dissonance of the rounds fired in such close quarters and fast succession exploded inside her ears.

And then the shots stopped.

A ringing silence filled the gap.

The scent of gun powder filled the small tent, the smoke rising from the barrel in swirling whiffs.

And she was still alive.

Her gaze flew to Josh. He was still there. Still on his knees. The 9 hung limp in his hand.

Beside her, Matthews crumpled to his knees and hung his head in defeat.

"Haskins. You did it! You killed it!"

He smiled up at her. His face ghastly white. His eyes unfocused. "Remember ... remember when you didn't tell me right away ... that we had to take Matthews ... alive?" he asked, his voice sounding strangely weak.

"Haskins?"

"I forgave you."

"Great. Fine."

"Now ..." He sank back on his heels. The gun slid out of his hand. "You have to forgive me ... for not telling you something."

Her heart nearly gave way when she saw blood dripping down out of his jacket sleeve and covering his hand.

"Haskins," she yelled and ran to him, catching him just as he collapsed.

"I'm ... Sorry."

She could barely hear him.

"I forgot to tell you. I ... I think I took a round."

"Damn you," she sobbed as he passed out in her arms. "Damn you. Don't you dare bug out on me now."

———

SHE HAD TO LEAVE HIM. She had no choice. He'd bleed out, or freeze to death if shock didn't kill him first.

Matthews didn't look so good either. Not that she cared. His eyes were closed, his breath short and shallow. If it was an act, it was a good one.

She couldn't wait any longer. She quickly flex cuffed Matthews to a metal brace supporting the bomb, far enough away from Haskins that he couldn't do any more damage. Then she rushed out of the tent and ran to Matthew's truck. It had been running when they got here but a round or two must have hit the engine block and it was stone cold dead now.

She scrambled frantically through the front then backseat looking for something, anything she could use to get the attention of the security guards – if the shots hadn't already alerted them.

"Thank you, Lord," she whispered when she found a flare gun and two flares tucked under the back seat along with a flash light.

She grabbed them and ran back into the tent. Wouldn't allow herself to look at Haskins. Not yet. She had to get the flares up.

As fast as she could work with her frozen fingers, she loaded the gun and stepped back out of the tent. Raising her arm high in the air and pointing in the direction of the plant, she fired off the first flare then watched as the red hot glow streaked through the air, leaving a trail of yellow vapor in its wake.

"Please let them see it," she whispered as she loaded the second flare and fired it off.

She watched for only a moment, knowing that they were Haskins' only hope.

Then she rushed back into the tent and ran straight to Haskins. His face was gray. His body shook uncontrollably.

"He's not going to make it," Matthews taunted.

"Shut up."

Holding back tears, she dropped to knees beside Haskins and wrapped herself around him. "You're okay. You're going to be okay. But you've got to fight. Please, please fight for me."

And there she stayed. Willing his cold, shaking body to absorb her heat. Praying someone would come in time. Dying with every one of his breaths – each one slower and more shallow than the other.

If he was going to die here, on this frozen, barren ground, pounded by this monster blizzard that seemed determined to kill them both, then she would die with him before she'd ever leave him.

CARA OPENED her eyes with a start. Sat straight up to a burst of shouts and the glare of spotlights surrounding the tent.

"Come out now! Hands in the air!"

Thank, God.

She rose on cold stiffened legs. Immediately raised her hands. "Coming out! I'm unarmed. We need help. Medical emergency."

When she stepped outside the tent, no less than twenty rifles and shotguns were leveled directly on her.

"On your knees! Hands behind your back."

"I'm Agent Cara Graves. RRA. Agent Joshua Haskins, RRA is down. He's been shot. He's lost a lot of blood. His condition is critical. Please, we need to get him inside. Triage his condition."

Not a single rifle budged.

"ID."

She lost it then. "Are you telling me you haven't already been notified that two RRA agents were on scene? That one of them was a woman?"

The leader of the group, a young man who took his job very seriously, looked a little sheepish but held his gun steady.

"Help us!" she demanded. "Get him inside before he dies or you can explain to RRA and your Commander in Chief that it was you, who let it happen!

"Oh, and they want this hostage alive, too," she snapped. "He's also going to die of exposure or blood loss if you don't do something fast."

"Hostage?"

"The bomber!"

"Bomb?"

She let out a frustrated breath. "Big bomb. That we took out of commission or you wouldn't be standing here right now letting the man who saved you die!"

One final concerned look, and he gave the order to stand down.

She only prayed that it wasn't too late.

"HE NEEDS A HOSPITAL. THEY BOTH DO."

Only out of a sense of duty did Cara give two rips about Matthews. But Haskins ... God, Haskins. He looked bad. Really bad. He'd never regained full consciousness after shooting the timer on the bomb.

He'd saved the world as we know it and didn't even know he was a hero. Well he was going to know. She was going to make damn sure that he lived to hear about it.

They'd plowed a path with the guard's trucks down to the complex gate and hauled both Haskins and Matthews inside. More guards met them at the door with thermal blankets and rolling desk chairs along with apologies that they had no gurneys.

Cara stayed at Haskins' side as they rolled him down a long hall, into an elevator, then out onto the cafeteria floor where they laid him carefully on a long table and started cutting off his outer wear.

"Cummings and Black are on the way with their kits."

Other than the guards, there were over three hundred people on each shift. Surely they had a doctor or a nurse on duty.

"Doctors?" she wanted to know.

"No, ma'am."

She spun around to see a thirty-something African-American man rushing into the cafeteria carrying a large kit.

"I'm an engineer here at the plant now. Eight years in the Army as a medic. Old habits," he said lifting his kit. "Never leave home without it. Let me see what I can do."

Her heart sank. "He needs a doctor."

"He does indeed," Cummings agreed as he started cutting away at Haskins' turtleneck. "I'll do my best for him. Can't let a hero die on my watch."

Because he looked and sounded so confident, Cara took heart.

"He dislocated that shoulder earlier," she told him. "He walked me through reducing it."

"Impressive." Cummings carefully moved Haskins' arm, searching for the source of the bleeding and blood spurted out of a wound on the inside of his upper arm.

"Damn," Cummings swore. "Bullet must have nicked an artery. I need you over here."

She scrambled to his side.

"Hold your fingers right here."

He positioned her fingers over the wound, made sure she applied enough pressure on it, then opened his kit. "Don't let off the pressure no matter what."

Haskins groaned and tried to pull away from her. She pressed her fingers tighter, then held his arm against his side and leaned over him, making sure she didn't lose her grip.

Cummings reached into his kit and came out with a tourniquet. She sensed his urgency as he quickly slipped it around Haskins' arm then tightened it above his elbow.

The bleeding stopped almost immediately.

"You can let go now," Cummings said. "It's okay," he assured her when she didn't move.

She was afraid to let go. Afraid she'd be responsible if he started bleeding again.

"It's okay," Cummings repeated softly and gently pried her hand away.

She crossed her arms under her breasts, oblivious to the blood from her hand staining her sweater. Then she almost passed out when she looked at Haskins' parka on the floor by the table. Heavily quilted fabric was bloated with blood. So much blood.

Haskins groaned in pain but didn't regain consciousness.

She looked at Cummings, frightened.

"That's a good sign," Cummings assured her again. "He's reacting to stimulus. His arm hurts like hell."

She needed a good sign. Because all of the signs she'd seen so far were bad.

Cummings bent down and retrieved the thermal blanket she'd let fall to the floor. When he placed it over her shoulders, she hugged it tight, only then aware that she was shivering.

"Get this lady some coffee," Cummings yelled to no one in particular. "Or would you prefer a shot of whiskey?" he asked quietly as he continued Haskins' physical examination. "I can rustle something up if you need it."

She managed a smile. "Oh, I need it. But I'll pass. Coffee will be great though.

"How is he? Really?" she asked because she couldn't stand it any longer.

Cummings checked his airway and breathing, then wrapped a blood pressure cuff around his other arm and pressed a stethoscope on the pulse inside his elbow and started pumping.

"He's strong," he assured her as he checked his pulse, his pupils and his respiration. "But I'll level with you. He's not in the best shape right now. He was exposed to the cold for an awfully long time. Although, it was the cold that probably helped keep him from bleeding out. If that bullet had pierced the artery instead of nicking it, he'd be gone."

"Oh, God," she reached for a chair. Sat down before her knees buckled.

Again, Cummings gave her a reassuring smile. "If we can keep his BP above 80, we can see him through until the ambulance arrives with plasma. In the meantime, I'm going to hang some saline. Always keep a couple bags in my kit."

At her alarmed look, he touched a hand to her shoulder. "Let's just be safe and not sorry, okay? We'll all be happier if he gets some fluid back in him. By the time the ambulance gets here, he should be fairly stable."

Ambulance. It just occurred to her. "How is an ambulance going to get out here through the snow?"

"Word is they've already put a couple of state snowplows back into commission. They're plowing their way out here as we speak. An ambulance is following them and they'll plow the ambulance back out and into Cedar Rapids and the hospital once we get him and the hostage loaded up.

"You two must really have some pull somewhere higher up."

She almost cried with relief to know that help was on the way. And yeah. RRA would put a lot of muscle into getting Haskins taken care of.

For the first time since she'd seen so much of his blood and realized how close to death he'd come, she thought about Matthews.

She hitched her head toward him. "Do you know anything about how he is?"

"Black's working on him over there. I'd say he's doing okay, though. No organs, no arteries involved. He's going to have a damn sore leg."

She glanced at the table behind her. Matthews was sitting up hunched under a blanket. His leg was wrapped and he was drinking hot coffee. Six of the plant's security guards stood watch, guns holstered but unsnapped and ready.

"Ma'am?"

She turned back and found a guard extending her a mug of steaming coffee.

"Thank you."

"You're welcome. Anything you need, you just let me know."

In that exact moment, she realized how exhausted she was. From worry about Haskins. From the cold. From the adrenaline crash after confronting Matthews and his men. The race to stop the bomb.

She thought back to the moment. Felt again, the tension of thinking that not only would she and Haskins be blown to red mist, but the bomb would destroy hundreds of thousands if not millions of people.

But they'd done it. They'd gotten here in time. Taken out Matthews' men. Taken Matthews down. Disarmed the bomb. Against all odds, they'd done it.

She hung her head and gripped her coffee with both hands trying to stop the tremors.

"You okay?" Cummings watched her with concern as he cleaned up Haskins' arm then pulled a blanket up over him.

She gathered herself, looked at Haskins, who had become restless suddenly. She set her coffee aside and went to him, helped Cummings hold him steady on the table, fussed with his blanket when he finally settled down.

"He really is going to be okay?"

Cummings nodded. "He's going to be fine. I'm still worried about you, though."

Relief came in the form of Cummings' confidence.

Haskins was going to make it.

She was still alive.

They'd done their job.

She smiled up at Cummings. "I'm okay. I'm really, really okay."

CEDAR RAPIDS 9 NEWS

December 24th
Christmas Eve morning

"It's like we've been telling you folks." Don McDowell smiled cheerily at the camera. "While Blizzard Holly blew in like a freight train and dumped record snowfall on north eastern Iowa, she strolled out with the manners of a lady, leaving a mess of melting snow and warmer weather in her wake."

Standing in front of the Iowa weather map, Don clicked his remote and brought up the current weather conditions. "We have record snow fall reported as far north as Decorah and as far east as Sabula but as you can see by the tallies on the map, the deepest snow recorded was right here in Cedar Rapids.

"We were lucky though. Only around 20,000 people were without power due to the strong winds. We can thank our hard working Alliant Energy crews for getting on top of it right away and power has already been restored to those folks.

"For Christmas Eve, we're looking at clearing road conditions as the State and County plows work overtime. By Christmas morning, we'll see blue skies, a balmy thirty-eight degrees and mild southerly winds."

He grew suddenly serious. "Holly may be gone, dissipating as she moves eastward, but it will be a long time before those of us in the KCRG TV 9 viewing area will forget her. A very long time.

"This is Don McDowell, signing off but not before we, at KCRG TV, wish you a very Merry and safe Christmas. Have a great rest of your evening and all day tomorrow."

EPILOGUE

"OH. MY. GOD." Cara sat up in the bed, pulling the sheet with her and laughed as Haskins strutted into the bedroom, wearing nothing but the straw hat she'd bought for him on the beach this afternoon, his medal, and a flirty smile.

"You're laughing at a hero, lady. Show some respect."

That made her giggle. "How about I show you a little skin instead?"

He gave the hat a toss. "Now you're talking."

He dove for the huge bed, landed beside her and propped his head on his hand. "Hello, wife."

She touched her hand to his hair. "Hello, husband."

It was the first day of their honeymoon in Fiji. Blue skies, sunshine, aquamarine water and sandy beaches. All of it was theirs for seven glorious days.

"Your shoulders are sunburned," he said and dropped a tender kiss on one then the other.

"Umm. I might have another spot or two that needs attention."

"I'm just the man for the job." He kissed her deeply. When he pulled away and met her eyes, his were suddenly serious. "I love you. I don't know if I can ever tell you how much."

She loved the look in his eyes. Knew the love in his heart was as true as love came.

Melancholy suddenly, she reached out and slipped a finger between his bare chest and the ribbon holding his medal. Lifted it so she could see how it shone in the soft bedroom light.

The medal was a match to hers. Just last week, two days before their wedding, they'd been honored for their heroics in the Palo incident. The medals had been placed around their necks by the president himself in a private ceremony at the White House with the scent of cherry blossoms wafting in through an open window.

No press attended. Everything possible had been done to conceal their identities and insure their faces and names would not be revealed. Their careers as RRA agents would be over if word got out.

The news about the thwarted attack on the Palo plant, and the tragic deaths of seven people, however, had made international news and had been in the headlines for over a week. Once Uri Avilov's identity was revealed and linked to dozens of other devastating attacks all over the world, the press got another week or more out of the mystery surrounding him.

Cara was sure someone would write a book about him.

The making of a terrorist.

Uri Avilov, international hired killer.

World's most wanted behind bars.

She sincerely hoped that if anyone profited from Uri Avilov's horrific acts, they'd dedicate some of the profits to the families of the seven innocent people who died in Cedar Rapids that night. If not for them, unknowingly bringing her and Haskins to Iowa, Avilov would have accomplished his deadly plan. And the world would be forever changed for the worse because of it.

She and Haskins had been referenced in the news reports only as 'highly skilled covert operatives' whose identities would remain undisclosed for their protection.

In the world of covert warfare, however, all the key players knew who they were and what they'd done. And after the medal presentation, RRA could hardly hold them to the 'no fraternization' clause since those same covert agencies had since tried to recruit them to be on their teams.

RRA didn't know it, but they didn't want to go anywhere. As long as they could do their jobs as husband and wife, RRA would be their home.

Her new husband pulled her away from her musings when he ran a finger along the curve of her breast. "Kind of hard to believe, huh?"

"That you'd strut into a room like a bawdy stripper?"

He wrapped an arm around her and pulled her close. "That six months ago we were almost vapor along with about a quarter of the country's population."

"Oh, that." She made a show of yawning in boredom.

He grinned then rolled on top of her and made her laugh again. "You have a wicked sense of humor Cara Haskins, spy extraordinaire."

"And?"

"And I think I love it." He stroked a hand through her hair.

"I think I love *you*." She lifted her head and kissed him. "Don't ever try to die on me again."

She had nightmares about that night. Woke up hyperventilating – seeing his blood everywhere but where it was supposed to be.

She'd stayed by his hospital bed day and night for fear he'd need her and she wouldn't be there. He'd spent three days in the hospital in Cedar Rapids until he was finally stable enough to be moved to Walter Reed Hospital where he stayed for another ten days.

He was fine now. His shoulder had healed. The wound in his arm had healed as well.

Had the bullet pierced his artery instead of nicking it – well, he wouldn't be alive. And she'd be existing in some dismal shadow of a world empty of everything but longing and loss.

"Hey ... hey, don't," he whispered, kissing the corners of her eyes where tears had gathered. It seemed he always knew when her mind went there. "I'm okay. We're okay. Together, we're indestructible."

When he was finally released from Walter Reed, a January thaw had set into not only the Eastern seaboard and most of the Midwest, but Iowa, as well, and the deep drifts they'd raced across on the snowmobile became mere memories.

"I'm sorry you didn't get to spend time with your family at Christmas."

"We'll make up for it next year." She held her wedding ring up to the light and admired it. "I got what I wanted."

"So did I," he murmured into her hair. "I got the girl."

He kissed her then and showed her with longing touches and tender love, how much she meant to him.

Later, after they'd napped and showered, they dressed for dinner. She was starving and looking forward to dinner at one of the outdoor restaurants where the tables were set with lush tropical flowers and only soft candlelight and tiki torches competed with the glow from the moon.

She'd put on a colorful sarong and pinned a fresh flower in her hair. And he – oh, wow. Haskins looked so healthy and gorgeous and tan in his white beachcomber pants, bare feet and island shirt.

"You want to be my cabana boy?" she asked playfully, meeting him in the center of their room.

He had a flirty look in his eyes when he drew her into his arms. "Depends on the duties."

"Oh, I think we can come to some terms that will satisfy both of us." She looped her arms around his waist, loving that he was hers now. Just as she was his.

"Thought maybe you might." He kissed her forehead.

"Are you ready to go? I'm starving."

"Looking at you ... how beautiful you are ... I'm ready all right. I'm ready to do some more dancing," he said with a sly grin.

She laughed. "I believe we've been *dancing* on and off all day, Haskins." She actually felt herself blush when he waggled his eyebrows. "That's why I'm starving."

"We'll get you fed in a minute. First, let's chat."

She laughed again. He never let go of a thing. "What do you want to *chat* about?"

"Glad you asked. Two things, actually."

"Only two?"

He took her hand and led her out to the veranda where the balmy ocean breeze washed over them. "You still have a secret."

She'd been afraid he'd bring that up again sometime.

"What did the team do to you for your initiation?"

"I was hoping you'd forgotten about that."

"Never."

She drew a deep breath. "You sure you want to know?"

"Am I going to want to punch someone's face in after I find out?"

She grinned. "It's a possibility."

Looking grim suddenly, he sat down on a lounge chair and pulled her onto his lap. "Tell me."

"Maybe it's better if we just leave that secret locked up for a while."

"Oh, no. You're not getting out of telling me. Now give."

"Just remember – it was all in good fun. And all about humility."

"Oh, I remember the humility part. I expected a critical first assignment and I ended up a glorified babysitter."

"Cute babysitter," she insisted.

"I'm waiting," he said. "Don't force me to torture it out of you."

"Hum. That sounds interesting."

"You asked for it."

She shrieked and squirmed when he started tickling her.

"Okay. Okay. Uncle!" Still laughing, she caught her breath. Then after a long, considering look, decided she'd just as well get it over with. Rip it off like a Band-Aid.

"They shaved my head, made me dress like a boy, and play house boy for them for a week."

He looked at her for a long moment. And he wasn't smiling now. Slowly his jaw clenched. "They shaved off your beautiful hair?"

"They did."

Another pause and if his narrowed eyes were any indication, he was royally ticked off. "Who are they?"

"Oh, no. That part I'll never tell. Because you probably *will* punch someone's face in."

"Like they don't deserve it? They humiliated you."

"And what did *Anastasia* do to you if it wasn't humiliation?"

He considered that for a moment. "True. But at least I got to look at her – make that you – during the week. Some of those dresses. Man. You tried me sorely, *princess.*"

"But you survived it. So did I."

He drew her toward him and kissed her. "You're an amazing woman."

"And you're an amazing man, Haskins. You said you had another question?"

"Yeah." Serious again, he looked her deeply in her eyes. "Could you just once, considering we're married and all ... call me Josh?"

THANKS FOR READING! **If you enjoyed this book, please do leave a review.**

Read on for a sneak peek of the first STORMWATCH novel, *Frozen Ground* by Debra Webb.

AUTHOR NOTE

Some of the towns, cities, and businesses I've used in this book are actual locations. I've taken liberties with all of them to make them 'fit' into my story line. None of the characters or events are real and any similarities with actual individuals or situations is purely coincidental.

SNEAK PEEK

FROZEN GROUND
STORMWATCH, Book 1
by Debra Webb

Camille Dutton pulled the hood of her extreme cold weather puff coat a little closer around her face. The temperature was barely holding at twenty degrees and would be dropping as the day progressed. Winter storm Holly was gearing up to wreak havoc. Camille shivered. What in the world had possessed her to move here? Livingston, Montana—Park County. Nature. Beauty. Cowboys. She exhaled a breath that fogged around her face. She'd fallen for a cowboy all right. He was the sheriff of Park County and totally unavailable except for the occasional date and doing his duty as a lawman. Garrett Gilmore was a lost cause. Oh well. This was only a stepping stone to a larger media market. Who knew? By spring she could be in Denver or Vegas.

"You're live in three, two, one," her cameraman warned, his voice a rough rumble against the wind whipping around them.

Camille fixed a grim expression on her face—not so difficult considering the worsening weather. "Brace for the worst, folks," she warned. "Winter storm Holly is bearing down on Park County. Holly has dropped enough snow across Washington and Idaho to spread a few inches over half the country. Property damage estimates are rising and, worse, the number of lives lost are mounting. This is not—I repeat, not—your typical Montana winter storm. This is the deadliest storm in nearly a century. Authorities are predicting that the Bozeman airport will be closed by early afternoon.

"Yellowstone's west gate as well as most other park gates on this side of Montana are being closed. Motorists are stranded all along the major interstates northwest of our viewing area. Please." Camille poured as much worry into her practiced voice as possible. "Please be careful out there. You have a few hours to gather any supplies you need and then you need to stay home. Believe me when I say, Holly will be on top of us before dark and she's leaving a trail of devastation in her path. Be careful, folks. And stay tuned into Channel 31. I'll be out here on the front lines keeping you advised of what's happening. This is Camille Dutton, Channel 31 News, back to the studio."

CHAPTER 1

Sunday, December 15
Park County, Montana

Abbey stood in the middle of the room and inhaled deeply. It was almost as if she could smell her father's aftershave.

She sighed. But that was impossible. Douglas Gray had died a year ago.

One whole year. It didn't seem possible. She'd just hit thirty and she had no family left. The image of her brother, Steven, filtered through her mind, but he had turned his back on her and what was left of their family years ago after what happened.

The *incident*.

Her father had insisted on referring to her mother's murder as the *incident*. It was easier that way, he'd said. What he'd meant was that if they didn't mention murder, they didn't have to talk about the trial or the fact that the accused was Steven—Abbey's brother, the son of the victim.

No matter that she and her father had struggled so mightily to get past what Steven had done and to hold together the shattered fragments of their family, her brother adamantly refused to communicate with them in any way after the trial ended. He'd been taken away in shackles and that was the last time Abbey had seen him. As hard as she and their father had wanted to believe his insistence that he was innocent, the evidence—an eyewitness for God's sake—had pointed to him. Still, they had both tried to see him, to talk to him, but Steven had refused. Year after year, their letters had been returned unopened. Eventually Abbey had stopped bothering; her father had as well.

Though she shouldn't, she couldn't help wondering how he was doing. Just before Thanksgiving last year the district attorney's office had called and conveyed the news that Steven had been released to a halfway house of sorts. The judge had been very specific with his sentencing. After his prison sentence was served, Steven would spend twelve months under close supervision, working and going to counseling, then he could move on with his life in whatever manner he chose as long as it was legal and as long as he reported monthly to his probation officer for another year.

So many times, Abbey had considered going to see him despite his past refusal to see her or to read her letters much less write back to her. In the end she had decided that if he could live without her, she could live without him in her life. Particularly after he hadn't bothered coming to their father's funeral. She'd made the necessary calls and felt certain he would have been allowed leeway to attend had he chosen to do so. It wasn't like he was that far away. Hardly more than two hours.

But he hadn't come or reached out in any manner—not even a sympathy card.

Frankly, until now, that was the last time she had thought about her brother.

Their father had left everything—which was the house and a hundred acres of land in the wilds on Montana—to her. His old truck, the tractor and various other personal property. She understood her father's reasoning for the decision, but she had not agreed with it. Once the property sold, she intended to put half of the proceeds into an account for Steven. He could take it or leave it. The choice was his.

Abbey shook her head. How was it that such a happy

childhood had turned into a stunning tragedy during their adolescent years?

"A dozen shrinks couldn't figure that one out," she muttered, pushing the disturbing thoughts aside.

She'd gotten in late last night. Too late to do anything but crawl into the bed she'd slept in the first eighteen years of her life. To make matters worse, she had promptly sunk into a dark, fitful sleep. She hadn't come to the family home since her father's funeral. He wasn't here, she really didn't want to be either. A maintenance service came once a month and took care of the place, inside and out. There was no reason for her to come...until now.

The insurance company had warned her that they would no longer carry a homeowner's policy on the house if it continued to be vacant. She had ninety days to sell or lease it or there would have to be changes to how she insured the property. Since she couldn't imagine ever wanting to live here again now that her father was gone, selling was the better option.

Before she could put the place on the market, there was a tremendous amount of work to be done. Going through a lifetime of what her parents had accumulated wouldn't be an easy feat, or a pleasant one. She would choose what she wanted to keep, and an auction company would come in and sell the rest. Sounded easy enough until she'd walked through the rooms, checking the closets and drawers. She had never really noticed the enormity of stuff her father had kept. Simple was not a word that described in any way the task ahead.

Before diving in, she needed coffee.

Unable to function without her caffeine fix, she had brought her coffeemaker and her favorite grounds. Thank goodness she had because the coffee in the cupboard was out of date—and instant.

The brew process had just finished as she walked into the kitchen. She poured a big cup and inhaled the amazing aroma. As she sipped the deliciously dark liquid, she gazed out the window over the sink. The sky had that look, the one her father always said meant snow was coming. She'd heard something on the radio those last few miles last night about a storm building up north, but she'd been too tired to pay attention. This was Montana, winter snow storms were a part of life.

She would be stuck here for a few days in any event so a snow storm wouldn't be such a bad thing. There was a generator. Beyond the window over the sink, her gaze roved the backyard from the house to the shed. The reassuring stacks of firewood would keep her comfortable for a good long while. Not a problem. As long as she had coffee, she would be perfectly fine.

Still, if there was a storm coming, she should likely have a look around outside now before the bad weather descended. A quick inventory of what her father kept in the shed and barn would be useful. She could take pics with her cell. Mr. Hansen, the closest neighbor, had sold the few horses and two cows her father had still owned when he died. The conscientious neighbor had been so helpful, he and his wife both, over the past year. Calling Abbey and giving her updates. Mr. Hansen—Uncle Lionel, he would insist—came over a couple of times a week on his daily walks to check on the house.

Her parents and the Hansens had been lifelong friends.

Abbey didn't really have any true lifelong friends. She'd left Montana to go to university to pursue her love of writing. After graduation she'd headed directly to New York to dive into the publishing world. She'd worked three years as an editorial assistant when her first completed novel was contracted by a publisher. Incredibly, her debut book had hit the New York Times bestseller list. Looking back, she was so grateful she'd been able to share that incredible recognition with her father before he was gone. He'd been so proud of her.

Currently she was in the middle of her second novel. Her publisher was chomping at the bit to get the next Abbey Gray thriller into bookstores. Unfortunately, Abbey was behind already and with all this to handle her deadline was looking less and less doable.

She'd brought her laptop along and hopefully she would get at least a little work done during this emotionally draining process.

After her second cup of coffee, she pulled on her coat, cap, gloves and boots before heading out the backdoor. The crisp morning air took her breath. New York winters could be brutal, but they didn't come close to the cold in Montana. Snow from the last dumping lingered here and there. Against a shaded corner of the house and the base of trees. Beyond the yard, in the woods there would still be a small drifts on the ground. Not once during her childhood could she ever recall wishing the snow away. She had loved it so much. She wasn't a kid anymore and life had shown her that all that lovely white stuff could be a real pain when there was work to be done, errands to run, appointments to make.

Last year while preparing for her father's funeral she hadn't really done anything but shower and sleep at her childhood home. She'd felt numb and in a fog. Garrett had been a huge help. She smiled. She'd been wrong before. She definitely had at least one lifelong friend. She and Garrett Gilmore had grown up together, gone to school together—though he was six months older than her. Everything in her life until she graduated high school and drove away without looking back had included Garrett.

Her first kiss. A wave of heat flushed her cheeks despite

the cold. They'd lost their virginities together. She laughed out loud at the memory. After weeks of thorough and logical consideration, the event had proven an awkward ten or so minutes.

The funny thing was, they had never actually felt the urge to be boyfriend and girlfriend. Best friends was a far better description of their relationship. The kiss and the sex—both of which only happened once, was about preparing for what came next. They had mutually decided that if their first experiences were going to be embarrassing, they would rather get them over with together. No one else would ever have to know.

She hadn't talked to Garrett since her father's funeral. He was the Park County sheriff now which meant he was very busy. During the past year her life had been one frantic book tour after the other. With all the publicity events and the movie option, she had been overwhelmed. Not that she was complaining. What author wouldn't love to have all this happen right out the gate with her first book?

She entered the combination for the lock on the barn door. Mr. Hansen had suggested the keypad locks to avoid issues with keeping up with keys. A really good idea under the circumstances. Like the house, the barn was reasonably well organized. Lots of tools and the tractor. Abbey turned on the lights and photographed the items for her own inventory. There was nothing here she needed. The auction company would, of course, do an independent inventory before moving forward. The shed was much the same. Stacks of firewood. Yard tools. The riding mower.

She stared across the yard and into the woods that stretched beyond the cleared space around the house. Voices whispered through her mind. Her father yelling. Blood everywhere. Steven swearing he didn't do it. Her mother's body lying on the frozen ground.

Abbey blocked the images and the sounds. Despite that horror, this place was peaceful and beautiful. Finding a buyer shouldn't be difficult.

Before turning back to the house, she made a last minute decision to visit the family cemetery. The stroll in that direction took her alongside the year-round stream that rushed through the woods as if fleeing for its life. Not once in her life did she recall it ever drying up. The path turned away from the water's edge and moved toward the small cemetery. Her father's parents were buried there as were her parents. She'd never known her mother's family. That set of grandparents had passed away when Abbey was very small. Her mother's one sister lived in Europe. The two had never been close.

A picket fence in need of a coat of paint surrounded the small cemetery. Abbey sat down on the stone bench her father had added after her mother's death. He would come here and sit for long minutes each evening. Life had been extremely difficult for him after the murder. He'd lost his wife and his only son. Abbey had felt as if she'd stepped into the twilight zone. Of course, she'd heard of a child murdering a parent but that was something that happened someplace else to someone else.

But it had happened to them. To her. To her world.

She stared at her mother's headstone. The trees shaded the small plot of land reserved for burying their dead, ensuring that snow lingered against the headstones. As a child she remembered thinking of how cold the graves must have gotten beneath all that snow each winter. By the time her mother was buried here, she had been old enough to understand the cold no longer mattered to those who resided inside this picket fence.

What she had considered as the snow had fallen that first winter after her mother's murder, was what her brother might be feeling and thinking as he sat in his prison cell. Had he been afraid? Lonely? Sad?

Abbey had sat through every hour of the trial. She heard all the testimony, the expert witnesses—all of it. Some part of her had never really believed her brother was the killer. Perhaps believe wasn't the right word. It was a sort of disconnect between what she was hearing and what her heart would allow her to absorb. Though he never said as much, she was certain her father had felt that same disconnect.

Steven could not have killed their mother.

Yet, the evidence and a single witness who had no reason to lie had insisted that he had, and the jury had concurred.

Enough with the trekking down memory lane. She stood and started back to the path. Another cup of coffee was in order and then she needed to get to work. The rasp of brush against brush had her stalling and turning toward the woods on her right. She listened for the crunch of icy snow or frozen leaves. The whisper of bare limbs against bare limbs.

Nothing.

There were any number of wildlife species running around in these woods. Her scent had likely stirred one or more. The place had been empty long enough for a sudden presence to prompt unrest. Nothing to worry about, she decided as she walked back to the house.

Inside, she peeled off the layers of protective outer wear and poured another cup of coffee, then checked her cell phone.

Maybe she should give Garrett a call. They could have lunch. Catch up. At some point during the arrangements and her father's funeral she had learned that he still wasn't married. A year later he certainly could be. She'd never been in a serious relationship, much less married. Focused, that had been her watch word. Get through college. Find the dream job. Write the book.

There hadn't been time for anything else.

Was time the real issue or had she still been drifting along in that personal fog? The part of her life that included intimate relationships on permanent pause? Had she ignored those needs to avoid having to deal with the *incident*? In truth, had she or her father ever really dealt with the ramifications of such a tragic loss and the stunning violence it had included? It was far easier to immerse herself in her studies and then her work.

Now here she was, thirty, alone and suddenly uncertain about too many things.

"Why the hell are you going there?" Abbey shook her head. Being in this house had her obsessing about the past.

She picked up her notepad and focused on what she should be doing. Making a list of the items she wanted to keep and of those she felt compelled to ship to Steven. So far there was nothing penciled in under either heading.

Upstairs, she went into her father's bedroom and began sifting through decades of his and her mother's lives. The odor of mothballs stirred in the closet. The clothes were all in good condition. Those could be donated. There wasn't any jewelry other than a few inexpensive pieces that had belonged to her mother. There was a pearl necklace Abbey intended to keep. She made a note of the item on her list but didn't find it in the jewelry box.

Considering her cramped apartment in Manhattan, she restrained her emotions and went for practical in her selections. She moved on to the en suite bath. A make-up table sat next to the pedestal sink. All these years, her father had left it exactly as it was the last time her mother had used it. The perfume she had worn, her few cosmetics, all sat exactly where she'd left them. Her father had never packed up any of her mother's things. Abbey opened the small center drawer to see if the pearls were there, but they were not. There was a brush and a handheld mirror, but no pearls.

She was certain she had seen them when she picked out her father's clothes for his funeral. They had been lying atop the jewelry box. Had someone from the maintenance company put the necklace up somewhere?

When she would have turned away from the vintage make-up table, she hesitated. Looked again. Something else was missing. The gold tube of red lipstick her mother had adored.

Abbey checked through the drawer again. Around the items on the top. Then she crouched down and checked beneath it.

The lipstick had been there last year. Since her father had already been dead the last time Abbey saw the gold tube lying on the table, someone else had moved it. Or taken it.

She would need to call the maintenance company.

The pearls she could see someone taking—although they weren't expensive pearls.

But why would anyone steal a tube of lipstick that was more than fifteen years old?*

THE STORMWATCH SERIES

Holly, the worst winter storm in eighty years...

Holly blows in with subzero temperatures, ice and snow better measured in feet than in inches, and leaves devastation and destruction in its wake. But, in a storm, the weather isn't the only threat—and those are the stories told in the STORMWATCH series. Track the storm through these six chilling romantic suspense novels:

FROZEN GROUND by Debra Webb, Montana
DEEP FREEZE by Vicki Hinze, Colorado
WIND CHILL by Rita Herron, Nebraska
BLACK ICE by Regan Black, South Dakota
SNOW BRIDES by Peggy Webb, Minnesota
SNOW BLIND by Cindy Gerard, Iowa

Get the Books at Amazon

ABOUT THE AUTHOR

Cindy Gerard is a New York Times, Publisher's Weekly, and USA Today best selling author. She's published over 50 books and received numerous awards, among them the RT's Reviewer's Choice and Pioneer Awards, the Daphne du Maurier Mystery/Suspense award, and two RWA Rita Awards. Cindy lives in the Midwest with her husband and a small menagerie of well-loved four-legged critters. You can find out more about Cindy's books at www.cindygerard.com.

ALSO BY CINDY GERARD

POCKET BOOKS:

ONE-EYED JACKS:
book 1: KILLING TIME
book 2: THE WAY HOME
book 3: RUNNING BLIND
book 4: TAKING FIRE

BLACK OPS INC STORIES:
book 1: SHOW NO MERCY
book 2: TAKE NO PRISONERS
book 3: WHISPER NO LIES
book 4: FEEL THE HEAT
book 5: RISK NO SECRETS
book 6: WITH NO REMORSE
book 7: LAST MAN STANDING

WORTH DYING FOR
WHEN SOMEBODY LOVES YOU

ST. MARTINS PAPERBACKS:
BODYGUARD SERIES:
book 1: TO THE EDGE
book 2: TO THE LIMIT
book 3: TO THE BRINK
book 4: OVER THE LINE

book 5: UNDER THE WIRE

book 6: INTO THE DARK

RESCUE ME - anthology with Cherry Adair and Lora Leigh

REISSUES: CLASSIC ROMANCE e-book only

CHARADE

RENEGADE

DREAM LOVER

WALK AWAY JOE

DON'T MISS

Printed in Great Britain
by Amazon

55588428R00128